"Are you near-death thing?" Ben said

"It's not a hang-up. After reading about other people's experiences, I'm more convinced than ever that it's real. So don't tell me I'm talking rubbish," Geena shot back.

"I wouldn't dare, but there are facts you should be aware of.... Apparently when the brain is starved for oxygen the neurons that deal with vision fire at random, creating the sensation of bright light. Because more neurons are at the center of our visual field and fewer at the edges, you get a tunneling effect."

She shook her head. "You don't understand."

"I'm trying to help *you* understand. All these so-called paranormal incidents can be explained scientifically."

She slung her bag over her shoulder. "Science doesn't have all the answers, Dr. Ben Matthews. Open your mind. You might be surprised at what flows in."

And then she was gone, hurrying around the corner. Ben gazed after her, shaking his head. Just when he thought he was beginning to know her, just when they were beginning to connect, some damn thing would blow up in their faces. If it wasn't her modeling, it was her near-death experience. Baby-sitting for a relative stranger, believing in the paranormal...studying *algebra*?

Who the hell was Geena Hanson, anyway?

Dear Reader,

Tales of near-death experiences have long fascinated me. Whether you believe they are a spiritual journey or merely the result of a lack of oxygen to the brain, there is no doubt that for many who undergo this profound experience, it is life altering. Among other things, love, in all its forms, becomes a reason for existence. As a romance writer, this seems to me only natural.

When supermodel Geena Hanson experiences near death after collapsing on a runway during a fashion show, she's no longer content with her materialistic lifestyle. Change is difficult and scary, but her newfound reverence for life helps her grow. When she falls in love with Dr. Ben Matthews, their opposing beliefs cause them to challenge each other on every level. Their conflict comes to a head over a young boy with cancer, whom they've both grown to love.

Child of Her Dreams is the second of three linked books about the Hanson sisters of Hainesville, Washington. Previously readers met Geena's eldest sister, Erin, in *Child of His Heart*.

I love to hear from readers. Please write me at P.O. Box 234, Point Roberts, Washington 98281-0234, or send me an e-mail at www.superauthors.com.

Joan Kilby

Child of Her Dreams
Joan Kilby

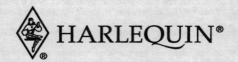

HARLEQUIN®

TORONTO • NEW YORK • LONDON
AMSTERDAM • PARIS • SYDNEY • HAMBURG
STOCKHOLM • ATHENS • TOKYO • MILAN • MADRID
PRAGUE • WARSAW • BUDAPEST • AUCKLAND

ISBN 0-373-71076-3

CHILD OF HER DREAMS

This edition published by arrangement with Harlequin Books S.A.

® and TM are trademarks of the publisher. Trademarks indicated with
® are registered in the United States Patent and Trademark Office, the
Canadian Trade Marks Office and in other countries.

Visit us at www.eHarlequin.com

Printed in U.S.A.

ACKNOWLEDGMENTS

While researching *Child of Her Dreams* I read, watched and listened to everything I could find on near-death experiences. Two items were particularly helpful: the book *Transformed by the Light: Life after Near-Death Experiences* by Cherie Sutherland, and the BBC series *The Human Body*, done by Robert Winston.

PROLOGUE

"BREATHE IN, *signorina*."

Geena sucked in her stomach, and the Italian seamstress wielded needle and thread to take a tuck at the waist of her ivory silk creation. Holding her breath made Geena feel even fainter; she hadn't eaten for two days in preparation for the launch of a new collection of Milan's hottest designer.

Throbbing techno music swirled through the dressing room as models returned from the catwalk, hurriedly stripping off one set of clothes in exchange for another. Geena's tightly strung nerves jittered with the warring effects of too many pills and too little food and sleep. She reached for another cigarette.

Lydia, her agent, glided over and ran a hand down Geena's back, pinching as though testing for flab. Penciled eyebrows lowered under a fringe of jet-black hair. "You look...fabulous, darling."

Geena tweaked the strands of her waifish coif and shook her head in self-disgust. "I need to lose five pounds before the Paris show."

"You seem on edge, Geena." Lydia eased the cigarette from between Geena's fingers and took a drag. "I've got plenty of girls for Paris if you want some time off at a Swiss spa."

Geena's heart raced at the thinly veiled suggestion that she wasn't needed. "I'm fine. Honestly."

"Think about it," Lydia said, blowing smoke over her shoulder as she drifted off to another client.

Geena's worried gaze followed her agent in the mirror. If Lydia wasn't insisting on her coming to Paris, if Lydia *wanted* her to take time out to go to a spa, Geena *must* be overweight. Maybe even on her way out.

Glancing at her image, she saw haunted blue eyes shrouded in gray and purple eyeshadow. Maybe Lydia wanted to replace her with some dewy-skinned teenager. At twenty-eight Geena was getting old to be a supermodel.

She was aware suddenly that her breathing was shallow and her rapidly beating heart had taken on an irregular rhythm. Please, no, not palpitations now; she was due on the runway in seconds.

She gulped air, trying to fill her lungs, scrabbled in her tote bag for a vial of pills and swallowed two with a gulp of mineral water. This was crazy. Forget Paris; after Milan she needed a break. After pushing her feet into a pair of four-inch heels, she made her way to the stage entrance.

The master of ceremonies detained her with a hand on her arm. "You okay, *signorina?* Your face, she is *blanca*—white."

Geena ignored the spinning in her head and gave him a brilliant false smile. "I'm fine."

She willed herself forward with an exaggerated sway of her hips and emerged into a blaze of klieg lights and popping camera flashes. Beneath the music and blinding lights she was uneasily aware of her erratic heart. For whole seconds she couldn't feel a beat. Then, just when she was sure she was about to die, blood thundered through the chambers as her heart raced to make up time.

She wanted to turn around right then, but the designer had paid big money for her to make an appearance. *Smile, Gee. You can do it.*

Midway down the catwalk, she faltered as pain traveled along both arms and a massive hand seemed to reach into her chest to squeeze her heart. She stopped dead and half turned, as if to go back to the dressing room. The next instant, everything went black.

Geena drifted upward, confusedly wondering where she was, what was happening. Below, a model lay facedown on the catwalk, long limbs sprawled awkwardly. A crowd had gathered around her, and people were shouting, gesticulating. Someone rolled the model over. With a jolt, Geena saw her own face staring unseeingly at her.

She was high above the room, floating among the klieg lights. Odd, she couldn't feel their heat. With detached interest she contemplated the hysterical urgency of the people trying to revive her. Some of the other models were crying. Excited shouts for a doctor yielded a small man in a black suit pushing his way through the crowd. Help was on its way, but it was too late.

She was dead.

The babble of voices formed a wall of sound that she turned away from, wanting peace. A tunnel appeared before her, and she went into the cavernous darkness, marveling at the soft, warm atmosphere. Then she was moving, traveling faster and faster through the darkness amid strange whooshing noises that came from nowhere. A pinprick of brilliant white light came into view. As she came closer the light grew larger and brighter, like the light of a trillion suns.

The light was good; she yearned toward it and eagerly allowed herself to be drawn in, for the light was love. Love and joy transcendent, bliss greater than anything she'd ever known. She felt incandescent, glowing with love and peace like the filament of a million-watt lightbulb. Was this a dream? Had doctors pumped some reviving drug into her veins? Perhaps any second she would wake up.

The light vanished.

She was in a small room with pale-green walls. Brown vinyl settees stood catercorner to an end table strewn with magazines and comic books. On one wall was a poster of a giant tooth being scrubbed by a cartoon dolphin, and in another corner stood an empty coatrack.

Geena looked again, and on one settee sat a woman reading a tattered copy of *Good Housekeeping*. She had long straight honey-blond hair parted in the middle, and her slim figure was clad in a seventies-style lime-green pantsuit.

The woman shut the magazine. Eyes glistening, she rose and reached out. "*Geena*. My baby."

"*Mom?*" Tears came to Geena as she was folded in loving arms. She was only three years old when Sonja Hanson had died, but deep in Geena's heart and mind was the indelible memory of her mother's scent, the loving timbre of her voice, the safety of her embrace. "Mom, is it really you?"

"It's really me." Sonja wiped away the moisture below each shadowed eye with a gentle swipe of her thumb. "Look at you, all grown up. You're so beautiful."

"Oh, Mom, we missed you so much—" Her voice broke. "All those years…"

Tears bled from her mother's eyes. "I missed you, too. You and your sisters. Don't cry, darling. Your father and I went to a better place. Truly."

Drawing back a little, Geena glanced dubiously around the little room. "Is this Heaven? It looks like a dentist's waiting room."

Sonja laughed softly. "No, it isn't Heaven."

"Then…oh, no, I've gone to the other place! Was it the pills? I swear I was going to get off them right after the Paris season."

Her mother shook her head, smiling sadly. "The pills helped send you to me, but we're not in the other place, as you put it. It doesn't exist."

"Limbo, then?"

Sonja smiled and took her by the hand. "Come, sit down and we'll talk."

Geena realized then that although they were communicating, no words had been uttered. She sat with her mother on the settee, hands linked with Sonja's, and let her thoughts flow outward. "Where's Dad? When can I see him?"

"I'm sorry, darling, that won't be possible. It's not your time."

"What do you mean? Aren't I staying here with you?" Now that she'd found her mother after being without her for so many years, losing her again seemed unbearable.

"I'm sorry," Sonja repeated. "You have important work left to do in life."

"Modeling?" Geena said bitterly. "It killed me."

Sonja brushed her fingers through Geena's wispy auburn bangs, as if she couldn't help touching her child. "A little glamour can lift people's spirits if not taken to extremes, but I didn't mean modeling."

Before her mother could say what she did mean, Geena had to ask the question that had preyed on her mind her whole life, even though she flinched from the painful memories of her parents' deaths and the aftermath of that dreadful night. "Mom, there's something I've always wondered about. Was Dad…drunk the night of the crash?"

"No," Sonja said firmly. "A dog leaped in front of the car. Your father swerved to avoid it and hit a patch of black ice. We skidded and crashed into a tree."

"I knew it. I mean, not about the dog, but we—Kelly, Erin, Gran and I—knew she couldn't be telling the truth." Sonja lifted her eyebrows, and Geena explained. "Greta Vogler planted the idea in everyone's mind that Dad went off the road because he was drunk.''

Sonja let out a deep sigh and squeezed Geena's hands. ''Try not to let Greta bother you. Forgive her if you can.''

''But *how,* when she—''

''Trust me, Geena, darling.''

Geena couldn't understand her mother's forbearance, but neither did she want to waste precious time talking about Greta Vogler. Heaven was simply being reunited with her mother. Geena could still hardly believe she was here, talking together as if they were sisters.

''I'm afraid it's time for you to leave,'' Sonja told her, as if aware of Geena's thoughts. ''You should go back to Hainesville.''

''Hainesville? What on earth would I do there?'' Yet even as she scoffed, the thought of returning to her childhood home filled her soul with a promise of peace. ''Maybe a visit would do me good.''

''Live there. People need you.''

Geena laughed. ''Me?''

''You have a talent for helping others. When you were little, you took in every stray that came your way.''

''Mom, that was long ago. Besides, I'm dead. How

can I help anyone? I want to stay here with you. I really want to see Dad. And Gramps.''

''It's not your time, Geena.'' Her mother hugged her again, then rose. ''You must go back.''

''No!'' Geena panicked as she realized her mother really meant it. ''Mom! Where are you going?''

Sonja opened a door on the far side of the room. Through the crack Geena glimpsed a rambling flower garden crisscrossed with swaths of lush green grass. In the fragrant center, a fountain burbled.

''Mom, take me with you. Don't leave me!'' Geena sobbed, as desperate as a three-year-old watching a coffin being lowered into the ground. *''Mommy!''*

Her mother returned to wrap her once more in her warm embrace. The light surrounded them both. Love, ineffable and infinite, poured through Geena as she clung to her mother.

''Geena, sweetheart, be brave. We will be together again someday, but for now you must go back.'' Sonja's voice was gentle, but again firm. ''A child needs you. You're going to be a mother.''

For the first time since Geena had arrived in this place, she felt utter disbelief. ''I can't have a baby. I haven't had a period in over a year.''

''Goodbye, darling,'' Sonja said, slowly backing away. ''Tell Gran that Gramps misses her. But he doesn't mind the wait. He has all the time in the universe.'' With that, she went through the door and disappeared around a cluster of flowering shrubs.

Geena found herself moving through the tunnel at dizzying speed, away from the light. The light faded to a pinprick. Once again, everything went black.

CHAPTER ONE

IN A SMALL VILLAGE in the western highlands of Guatemala, Dr. Ben Matthews listened to the agitated outpouring of a Mayan Indian woman who clutched her ailing baby boy to her breast. Ben understood only a few words of her native language, but the source of her worry was unmistakable. "I'll have a look at him."

He rolled up the sleeves of his white cotton shirt, gently took the child from the mother's arms and laid him on the examining table. The baby's hot, dry skin, sunken eyes and dry mouth all pointed to severe dehydration. Using a combination of sign language, formal Spanish and a smattering of the local dialect, Ben questioned the mother. She confirmed his suspicions; the child had vomiting and diarrhea.

"Dysentery," Ben explained. "He needs fluids."

The mother nodded mutely, then watched anxiously as Ben prepared an electrolytic solution and hooked up an IV to let it drip into the baby. The poor tyke was too sick to cry at the needle or to laugh when Ben tickled him under the chin. Ben's heart clenched. Two years of treating people ravaged by disease, malnutrition and poverty had not inured him to the heartbreak of a high infant mortality rate. This little boy had a chance, at least.

Ben gave the mother several packets of electrolytic solution. "Mix with boiled water," he said, miming what she was meant to do with them. "Baby drink."

She nodded again, then wrapped her baby and placed him in a colorful woven sling across her back. With a grateful smile that needed no words to be understood, she took her leave. From the doorway Ben watched her bare feet squelch through mud till she got to the hard-packed dirt road on a journey of perhaps many miles to her village.

Turning, he glanced at his watch, and his spirits lifted when he saw that the bus from Guatemala City would arrive soon. Eddie, his younger brother, had just finished his internship and at Ben's urging was going to replace him here at the clinic funded by International Médicos.

Ben strolled through the narrow streets lined with two-story adobe houses to meet the bus, greeting villagers with a smile and a wave, sometimes pausing to ask after a sick relative. Underlying his eagerness to return to the United States was a sense of loss at the prospect of leaving the town and its people behind.

The gray clouds building overhead distracted him from the excitement of seeing Eddie. July was smack in the middle of the rainy season, and this year had been unusually wet. Ben's main concern was the mosquitoes the river bred and the diseases they carried—malaria and dengue fever. But there were other dangers. The river was already high and threatening to flood its banks.

The bus arrived in a festive blare of marimba music spilling through open windows and lurched to a halt outside the cantina. Passengers spilled out. Ben searched the assemblage—Mayan Indians, Ladinos, backpacking travelers—and the odd goat—for his brother.

Eddie stepped off at last, dazed, his arms wrapped around a duffel bag and a backpack slung over his shoulders. His blond hair was mussed and his clothes wrinkled, as though he'd slept in them, which Ben knew he probably had.

"Eddie, over here," Ben called, striding toward him.

Eddie saw him and dropped his duffel bag in the dirt so that Ben could embrace him in a fierce hug.

"Great to see you, buddy," Ben said, leaving one

arm draped over his brother's shoulder. "How was the trip?"

"Interesting." Eddie pulled a downy chicken feather from his hair. He looked at it, then at Ben, and grinned. "I can't believe I'm here."

"Believe it, bro." He ruffled his brother's hair. "Better cut that mop or you'll find worse than chicken feathers in there."

"Oh, yeah?" Eddie punched him in the ribs. "What's with the face rug? Wait'll Mom sees that."

Ben stroked his carefully clipped mustache-and-goatee combo, smiling through his fingers. "I kind of like it. Gives me a certain polish, don't you think?"

He picked up the duffel bag and started walking to the clinic, weaving through rusted-out cars, bicycles, mule-drawn carts and pedestrians. "How are Mom and Dad? Did you get to Austin to see them before you left?"

"Yep. They send their love. They're looking forward to having you Stateside again, but aren't too happy with you for dragging me down to this mountain wilderness."

Ben gazed around him, at the Spanish colonial architecture, the Mayans in their colorful native dress, the pine-covered Sierra Madre. "I'll never forget my stint here. It's been a fantastic experience that I wanted to share with you.''

"I'm not complaining," Eddie said. "This is the opportunity of a lifetime.''

"Dr. Ben! Dr. Ben!" A ragged group of five or six children ran alongside the two men as they moved through the crowd.

"Hey, kids." Ben broke his stride and gestured to his brother. "Dr. Eddie," he said, then added a few words in the local dialect.

"Dr. Eddie!" The children crowded around him, touching his hand or his sleeve. Then they laughed wildly and ran away down the street, scrawny dogs chasing at their heels.

"What did you tell them?" Eddie asked with a wary grin.

"That you were my brother.''

"That's obviously a recommendation. I hope I can live up to your reputation.''

Ben eyed him with affection. He almost wished he hadn't urged Eddie to come here; he'd missed him, and now their separation would be prolonged further. "I've gotten attached to these people, especially the kids, but I feel better knowing they'll be in good hands.''

"Thanks." Eddie looked beyond the rooftops into

the distance, at the cone-shaped mountain rising above the plain. "That a volcano?"

Ben nodded. "Volcán Santa Maria. It's considered active. The region is also prone to earthquakes. We've had a couple of mild quakes during my time here but nothing to write home about."

Ben stopped in front of the clinic, a low white-washed adobe building with chickens pecking in the yard. A sign beside the door displayed a large red cross and the words International Médicos.

"Here we are." Ben pushed open the door. "Clinic out front, residence in back. It's simple, but it's home."

Eddie wandered through the clinic, surveying the meager shelves of medical supplies, the primitive equipment. "It's a change from a big-city hospital," he admitted in massive understatement. "What are some of the health issues you deal with?"

Ben perched on the edge of the small desk in the corner. "Oh, God, where to start. There's dysentery, insect-borne diseases, outbreaks of cholera and hepatitis. Malnutrition is a big problem, especially among the children. I spend most of my stipend providing food for hungry kids." He shook his head. "Infant mortality is high. No matter how hard you try there's so much to battle—disease, poverty, ignorance." As he thought of some of the little ones he'd lost, his voice became unsteady. "I *hate* it when the children die."

He pushed off the desk and moved across the room. "There are bright spots, reasons for optimism. I've set up a vaccination program, one for oral hygiene, and on Tuesdays and Thursdays I travel to the more remote villages and treat those who can't come to me.

"Come and see where you'll be living." Ben pushed aside a curtain of woven fabric in deep blues and reds and led the way into his private quarters. One end of the room was fitted with a hot plate, fridge and sink, while the other end held a single bed that doubled as a couch, a bookshelf crammed with paperbacks and, Ben's pride and joy, a turntable and speakers he'd picked up in Guatemala City to play his record collection. He put on Harry Connick, Jr.

"Man, our musical tastes never did coincide," Eddie complained. "Don't you have any Shaggy or New Radicals?"

Ben wrapped him in a headlock. "No, but I've got a cold beer. Want it? Say uncle."

"Piss off." Eddie hooked a foot behind Ben's ankle in an attempt to bring him down, but he was laughing too hard.

Ben released him and went to the fridge, a relic of the fifties, and reached past shelves of medicines for a couple of long-necked brown bottles of Guatemalan beer. He flipped the caps off and handed one to Eddie. "Luckily for us, doctors have to store medicine. Refrigeration is a perk of the job."

"Is that a fridge benefit?" Eddie asked, raising an eyebrow wryly. He unstrapped his backpack and pulled out a bottle of duty-free Jack Daniels and a newspaper. "Care for a taste of home?"

Avid for news, Ben bypassed the bourbon to pick up the recent copy of *USA Today*. The headline story blared in inch-high black print: Supermodel Collapses on Milan Runway—Miraculous Return From the Dead.

A photo, obviously taken before the model's collapse, showed her draped in designer clothing and glittering with diamonds against a backdrop of an Italian palazzo.

"Will you look at that?" Ben said, shaking his head in disgust. Evidence of excess always raised his ire on behalf of his poverty-stricken patients. "That dress alone would likely supply vaccine for the whole western highland. Look how thin she is. No wonder she collapsed. I'll bet she pops diet pills as if they were candy, then lets men take her to expensive restaurants and doesn't eat. Meanwhile, kids here are literally starving."

Eddie glanced over his shoulder at the newspaper. "She doesn't look too good now."

It was true. Below the first photo was an after shot of the woman in a hospital gown whose voluminous folds accentuated her prominent bones and gaunt features.

Like death warmed over, Ben judged grimly, and felt a spark of compassion. As ill as she looked, her beauty shone through, ghostlike and fragile, and something about her face compelled his attention. The farseeing expression in her tilted blue eyes seemed to hint at some profound knowledge. Life, the universe and everything, to quote a favorite author from his med-school days.

Losing interest, Eddie went to sprawl on the couch. "What else can you tell me about the place?" he asked, sipping his beer.

Ben tossed the paper aside, dismissing his ruminations as fanciful. A woman like that probably didn't have two ideas to rub together, let alone any magic answers.

"Let's see…" He sat on a wooden chair and tilted back at a precarious angle, sipping his beer. "Quezaltenango is the nearest big town—most Anglos around here refer to it as Quez. There are quite a few ex-pats scattered over this general area, a French doctor a couple of villages away, some nurses, teachers, agricultural aid workers, missionaries. You won't lack companionship.''

"Hey, you don't need to sell it to me. If you like it so much, how come you're leaving?" Eddie asked.

"For one thing, International Médicos stipulates a maximum two-year contract, which you should know having just signed on. For another thing…"

Ben pushed to his feet and stood before the window. "I had a thing going with this British nurse, Penny. She was only here for a year. We both knew from the beginning it wasn't going to last."

"So what's the problem?"

Ben shrugged and faced Eddie. "I'm tired of moving around, tired of temporary liaisons. I'm thirty-five. I'm ready to settle down."

"Will you go back to Texas?"

"No, I've arranged a temporary job through a guy I went to med school with. He's at Seattle City Hospital now and knows a GP in a small town north of there who's looking for someone to take over his practice while he goes on sabbatical. Hainesville. Ever heard of it?"

Eddie thought for a moment then shook his head. "It's probably just a dot on the map."

Ben laughed. "As opposed to *this* bustling metropolis. The first thing I'm going to do when I get back is buy myself a hamburger with everything on it and a great big chocolate milk shake.'' He turned to the window, filled with yearning for the good ol' U.S. of A. ''I don't know why, but I have a feeling Hainesville will suit me just fine.''

''HAPPY BIRTHDAY to you, happy birthday to you...''

Geena basked in the glow of the candlelit faces around Gran's kitchen table as her sisters and their families helped her celebrate her twenty-ninth birthday. There were Kelly and Max and their four daughters, and Erin and Nick with Erin's baby son and Nick's teenage daughter. And of course Gran, looking smaller than Geena remembered, in her full gray wig and oversize blue plastic glasses but fighting fit despite her seventy-six years.

A month had passed since Geena's collapse. She'd spent a week in the Milan hospital, followed by two weeks in a Swiss convalescent home, then a week in New York to pack her things and sublet her apartment. Finally, she was home, and it felt good.

Geena made a wish and blew out the candles. Everyone cheered. Kelly gave Geena an impromptu hug, her shiny brown hair swinging around her shoulders. ''It's good to have you with us, Gee, especially for your birthday.''

''What did you wish for, Auntie Geena?'' asked Beth, Kelly's eight-year-old daughter.

"Can't tell, or it won't come true," Geena said, smiling as she cut the cake and passed it around. Gran opened the curtains, and afternoon sun poured in. Erin tucked her long blond hair behind her ears and attempted to dish out ice cream one handed while holding the baby.

"Let me take Erik," Geena said, and reached for her nephew. She cuddled the baby in the crook of her arm and stroked the back of her finger down one soft cheek. "Hello, gorgeous."

Magazine publishers paid thousands for Geena's smile, but to her, Erik's toothless grin was priceless. His innocent blue eyes, so trusting and sweet, stirred her maternal instincts. Would her wish—and her mother's prediction—come true?

"Do you want chocolate or vanilla ice cream with your cake, Geena?" Erin asked, holding the scoop poised above the tubs of Sara Lee.

"Nothing for me, thanks." She'd already pigged out on green salad and half a grilled chicken breast.

"What? Not even cake?"

"I'm going back to modeling once I've recovered completely. I can't afford to gain weight."

"But, Geena," three-year-old Tammy said. "You're skinnier than a Halloween skeleton."

Kelly, who'd taken over serving the cake, frowned

across the table at Tammy. "Shh, honey, that's not polite."

"It's okay, Kel. She only wanted to make me feel better. Didn't you, sweetie?" she said, stroking the girl's long blond hair.

Geena saw her sisters exchange glances, and an awkward silence fell over the group. What the heck was bugging everyone?

Nick swallowed the last of his cake and pushed back from the table. "Hey, Max, want to go shoot a few hoops?"

"Sure thing." Max, Kelly's husband, set aside his empty plate. "It's been a while since I whupped your ass."

"Take your cake outside to the picnic table, girls," Kelly said, shooing her brood through the back door.

Miranda, Erin's stepdaughter, hovered in the doorway. At thirteen she often got lumped with the other kids when she wanted to be one of the women. She had auburn hair and a tiny stud in her nose.

"Come and sit down," Geena said, patting the chair next to her.

Miranda, who was into clothes and adored her supermodel aunt, threw her a grateful smile. "Thanks."

Erin set Erik in his car carrier seat and found a

rattle to amuse him. Gran took up her knitting from the sideboard, and Kelly, never one to sit still for long, started to clear away dishes.

"Relax, Kelly," Geena said. "I'll do that later."

"I don't mind," Kelly said, stacking plates in the dishwasher while the water ran in the sink for the pots from their barbecue lunch. Geena, realizing that Kelly wouldn't sit down, got up to help.

"Have you seen the doctor yet, Geena?" Erin asked, spooning up the last blob of chocolate ice cream from her plate.

Geena searched the drawers for a tea towel. "No, I'll make an appointment with Dr. Cameron tomorrow."

"Dr. Cameron's in Australia till Christmas," Miranda informed her dolefully.

"Dr. Cameron's son, Oliver, is a good friend of Miranda's," Erin explained to Geena. "She misses him."

"Just don't get too serious, too soon," Kelly warned Miranda over her shoulder as she vigorously scrubbed the potato pot. "Or before you know it, you'll have kids and you'll wonder where your girlhood went."

"We're just friends," Miranda protested. "Anyway, you and Uncle Max were childhood sweethearts."

"Exactly." Kelly rinsed the pot and handed it to Geena. "I hear the new doctor is quite a hunk. Indiana Jones with a stethoscope."

Miranda snorted disparagingly. "Dr. Matthews is *way* better looking than Harrison Ford."

"I've spent enough time around doctors lately, thanks very much," Geena said. "Not that I'm not grateful to them for saving my life."

"What actually happened to you in Italy, Gee?" Erin asked. "You've hardly told us anything. It was a heart attack, right?"

Geena wiped the pot dry, marveling that she could take pleasure in mundane chores. "My heart stopped. Apparently I was clinically dead for two minutes." Laughing, she rapped her skull with her knuckles. "No brain damage—at least, not that I can tell."

Kelly shivered. "It must have been awful."

"Not entirely," Geena said slowly, looking from Kelly to Erin to Gran. She hadn't told them about her near-death experience. She wasn't sure what their reactions would be. She wasn't sure how *she* felt about it. The experience had changed her in ways so subtle she hadn't yet fully grasped their significance. Every morning she woke up with a great gladness to be alive. And sometimes she stopped in the middle of whatever she was doing and looked, really *looked,* at what was around her. As if the world was brand-new. Or she was.

But something in her voice had captured the others' attention, and now all eyes were on her. Geena took a deep breath. She might as well tell them. "I had a near-death experience. I went to the other side and came back."

"What!" Erin and Kelly exclaimed together.

At the abrupt sound, Erik awoke with a jerk, one hand flung quivering in the air. Miranda's eyes went round. Gran's eyebrows rose above the wide plastic frames of her glasses, and the click of needles fell silent as she paused, yarn looped around her index finger.

Erin picked up her baby. "Don't cry, honey," she cooed, then turned to Geena. "Do you mean, as in flying through a tunnel toward a bright light?"

"Yes! It was so amazing I can hardly describe it." Words tumbled from her lips at the relief of finally sharing her experience. "I didn't know what was happening at first, not until I saw my body lying below me. There was darkness and I was moving through a tunnel toward a light. Everything—past, present and future—was there in the tunnel. All around me was a noise, a kind of icy sizzle, like moonbeams hitting water, if you know what I mean."

Their blank stares told her they didn't. Geena frowned, frustrated at the effort of describing something that couldn't be described in words. "The light was brighter than any sun," she went on. "As I got closer to the light I experienced an intense feeling of peace and love, joy and rapture and gladness and…" Her arms were uplifted when she ran out of breath. "Bliss. Pure bliss."

"Were you…on anything at the time?" Erin asked carefully.

Geena dropped her arms. "What do you mean?"

"Were you taking any…medication?"

"I'd been on diet pills," Geena admitted. "I use sleeping pills occasionally. And sometimes pills to wake me up."

"Pills to make you feel good?"

Geena crossed her arms over her chest. "*No.* I didn't have this experience because I was drugged."

Gran tugged some yarn loose from the ball on the floor, and her cat, Chloe, a blur of blue-gray fur, leaped from behind a chair to attack it. "I read an article once about a woman who had a near-death experience during heart surgery," Gran said. "Sounded pretty similar."

"Thank you, Gran." Geena relaxed her fists.

"Geena, honey, we love you. We didn't mean to

imply anything,'' Erin said. Kelly nodded in silent agreement.

But Geena could see they were still skeptical.

''Anyway, I'm off all those pills. I quit smoking, too. The doctors made me go cold turkey in the hospital.'' She sighed as she looked at herself. ''I've been gaining weight ever since.''

''It's good you quit smoking.'' Erin paused. ''But as far as your size goes, Tammy was right, you've *lost* weight. You weren't even this thin two months ago at my wedding.''

Geena did *not* want to get sidetracked into discussing her weight. She adored her sisters, but they didn't understand the pressures a model was under. Besides, she still had the most important part of her story to tell.

''I saw Mom,'' she said, almost defiantly. ''She said to give her love to all of you.''

''Geena, when you say you saw Mom, you mean as in a dream, right?'' Erin said. Erik stirred in her arms, and she reached under her blouse to unhook her nursing bra.

Geena watched her sister adjust Erik at her breast, and her heart clenched with longing. She wanted to tell them about the baby Mom promised she would have, but then Erin and Kelly would think she was completely nuts. Sometimes when she thought of the baby, even *she* wondered if she hadn't imagined the whole experience.

"It was as real as being here with you today. She told me it wasn't my time and that I had to go back. Well, she didn't actually speak. It was more like telepathic communication."

"Telepathic," Kelly repeated skeptically.

"She also said Dad wasn't drunk the night they died," Geena said, ignoring her. "They swerved to avoid a dog."

"That's the first we've heard of a dog," Erin said. "It's plausible, but impossible to prove."

Geena blinked. "Do I have to *prove* this happened?"

"Of course not. But you've got to admit, it's a bit far-fetched. You've been under a lot of pressure. It would be natural for your mind to play tricks on you," Erin said. "Maybe you should talk to the doctor, see what he says."

"I might just do that." A doctor was bound to have patients who had experienced near death and lived to tell about it. A doctor would reassure her she wasn't imagining things.

"How long are you staying?" Erin asked, raising Erik to her shoulder to pat his back. "I hope you're not going to flit off too quickly. We miss you."

"I'll be around for a few months. I told my agent

not to accept any new jobs until I've fully recovered.'' The truth was, she felt a little confused about her future direction, but the fashion industry was all she knew.

Kelly drained the sink and dried her hands on a towel as she glanced at the kitchen shelf clock Erin had left behind for Gran when she'd married Nick. ''Gosh, look at the time. I'd better get my kids home. Geena, come over for dinner real soon. My lasagna will put some meat back on your bones.''

Geena hugged her sister, knowing she meant well. ''Thanks, Kel.''

Erin carefully lifted her drowsy baby against her shoulder and gave Geena a one-armed hug. ''I'd better go, too. Erik always sleeps better in his own crib. Take care of yourself, Gee. We've been so worried about you. We want you to get completely well.''

''I will, don't worry.''

Geena walked them to the door and waited until Erin and Kelly had rounded up their families, bundled all the children into their respective cars and driven away. After they left, she sat on the painted wooden steps of Gran's big old Victorian home, the home she and her sisters had grown up in after their parents had died.

Scents of late summer wafted on a warm breeze— roses; mown grass; a whiff of salt from the river telling her the tide was in. The heavy crimson head of a poppy drooped through the railing, and she stroked a silken petal with her fingertip, lost in admiration of its beauty.

Hearing a sound behind her, she glanced over her shoulder to see Gran coming through the open door.

Gran lowered herself to the top step, her knees creaking a little in her track pants. "Tell me more about your mom. Did she seem happy?"

Thank God for Gran. "She's happy. So is Dad. Mom sent a message from Gramps that he'll wait for you forever."

Behind her glasses, Gran's pale-blue eyes misted.

CHAPTER TWO

BEN GLANCED AROUND the Hainesville Medical Clinic with satisfaction. With two examining rooms, a small lab, office, reception area and waiting room, the clinic was positively luxurious compared with what he'd been used to in Guatemala.

The only glitch was that he hadn't been in his new job a week before the nurse-receptionist who had worked for Dr. Cameron had been called to the sickbed of her elderly mother in Florida. Ben contacted an employment agency and was promised a temporary replacement in a couple of days.

Meantime, he took the loss in his stride; he'd coped with far more calamitous events in Guatemala. However, his patients were less sanguine than he about mixed-up appointments and general administrative confusion. Nor were they content to sit and wait for hours on a first-come, first-serve basis like his stoical villagers.

"You can't run this clinic the way you ran that place in Central America," a pinched-faced woman with tight gray curls told him after he'd inadvertently double booked her with the mayor. The mayor, Mr. Gribble, had won on the basis of having to attend an important meeting with the bank manager. Strangely enough, when Ben glanced out the window afterward, he'd seen Mr. Gribble heading for the river, with a fishing rod propped in the back of his Cadillac.

"Why not, Mrs. Vogler?" He began to scan the long medical history in her file to bring himself up to speed on her background.

"It's *Miss* Vogler. We're not a bunch of Mayan Indians, you know."

More's the pity.

"Dr. Cameron never did things this way. And where's your white coat?" Greta Vogler added with an accusing glance at his Guatemalan shirtsleeves and clean khaki pants. "If it wasn't for that stethoscope around your neck, no one would know you were a doctor."

"Unless they happened to notice the diplomas hanging on the wall," Ben said pleasantly, still reading. He came to an entry and paused. "It says here you had a hysterectomy in nineteen-seventy-six." He gazed at her, mentally calculating. She would have been in her midtwenties at the time. "Could this date be a mistake?"

"There's no mistake," she said frostily, looking away. "But what that has to do with the migraines I came to see you about, I don't know."

"My apologies," he murmured, and decided to skip the rest of the history. "Tell me about the headaches," he said, and went on to deal with that.

That was yesterday. Today, he'd hit upon the idea of stacking patients' files in the order in which they had phoned in for an appointment. When he got a call, he located the appropriate file from the filing cabinet and placed it at the bottom of the growing stack. He gave people a rough estimate of when they would see him, knowing no one ever expected to get in to see the doctor exactly on time. Simple yet effective.

Midmorning, Ben strode to the reception desk and leaned across it to pick off the top file so he could call in his next patient. But his eyes were on his watch instead of what he was doing, and he misjudged the distance. The entire stack of manila folders went slithering to the floor while the waiting patients watched in dismay.

Ben muttered a mild Mayan imprecation and crouched to pick up the files. A moment later a young woman with chin-length auburn hair left her seat to help him.

"You need an assistant," she said, stacking manila folders randomly in the crook of her arm.

"I know I do. I registered with an employment agency, but so far they haven't found anyone suitable."

"Then maybe you should look for someone unsuitable."

The smile in her voice made him glance up, into deep blue eyes that tilted, almond shaped, at the corners. Too slender for his taste, she was nevertheless undeniably attractive.

She was also vaguely familiar. "Have we met?"

She held his gaze with a bemused expression. "I would have remembered if I'd met you."

"I never forget a face," he persisted. "I'm sure I've seen you somewhere."

She shrugged, glanced at the files in her arm and rearranged them. Then she placed her files atop his. Ben rose and held his hand out to help her to her feet. Her height surprised him. She had to be five-ten in her stockings, and the heels she wore put them on eye level.

He looked around the room, reading the name off the top file. "Geena Hanson?"

"That would be me," said the blue-eyed woman, smiling, and she sauntered gracefully ahead of him to the examining room.

"Used to getting our own way, are we?" he said as he shut the door. Her clothes, her perfume, her very demeanor, shrieked wealth and sophistication. For some reason he thought of Penny, his British nurse, caring for peasants in jeans and T-shirt.

Geena Hanson took a chair and crossed one very long leg over the other. "I was next."

"I see." He opened her file and began to read the contents. "So, what seems to be the trouble?"

"Nothing, as far as I'm concerned."

Ben ignored her blasé answer and perused her recent medical history. His frown deepened as he read about her collapse in Italy and the two minutes during which her heart had stopped. A memory of newspaper headlines clicked in his brain. "You're that supermodel. What are you doing in Hainesville?"

"This is my hometown. I'm recuperating. Is that a Texas accent?" she inquired.

"I'm from a small town outside Austin." Ben went on reading, shaking his head at the recorded cocktail of pills she'd been taking and at her weight. His first impression was confirmed; she was unhealthily thin. And in denial about her problems.

Hands steepled over her file, he eyed her appraisingly. "If there's nothing wrong, why are you here?"

She inspected her perfectly manicured nails. "My

sisters and my grandmother insisted I get a follow-up examination.''

"Are you still taking these tablets?''

"No. I quit smoking, too.''

"Sleeping okay?''

"Could be better. But without five a.m. starts and late nights I'm getting by.''

"Any significant events following your collapse?'' he asked, jotting notes with his fountain pen.

She didn't answer right away, and he glanced up to see an odd light in her eyes. She leaned forward, clutching her Gucci handbag. ''What exactly do you mean?''

Instinct told him something important was in the air, but he had no idea what. ''Palpitations, dizziness, chest pain…''

"Oh.'' She leaned back, seemingly disappointed. ''I get a little dizzy sometimes first thing in the morning.''

Ben waited, giving her a chance to elaborate. When she didn't add anything, he asked, ''The dizziness—do you get it before breakfast or after?''

"I don't eat breakfast.''

All the advantages of money and position and not a lick of sense. He sent her a stern cold look. ''It's time you started. You're significantly underweight.''

He rose and came around his desk. "Hop onto the examining table."

He checked her blood pressure, pulse and reflexes. He peered into her ears, shone a light in her eyes and felt the glands below her jaw. As his examination progressed he became increasingly aware of her as a woman, something that was *not* supposed to happen. But his senses could no more exclude the elusive scent of expensive perfume and the porcelain texture of her skin than they could miss the beat of her pulse beneath his fingertips.

Perspiration dampened his armpits as he slipped his stethoscope beneath the scoop neck of her silk dress. What should have been routine had become mildly erotic. She went very still, as if she was aware of him, too.

"Your, uh, heart rate's a little fast." This was crazy; she was *not* his kind of woman.

"White-coat syndrome?" she suggested with a whimsical lift of her eyebrows. She'd brushed them upward, and their lushness emphasized the deep lapis blue of her eyes and the delicate bridge of her long straight nose.

"I'm ordering some follow-up blood work," he said briskly, retreating to his desk to uncap his fountain pen and fill out the correct form. "I understand the hospital down the road in Simcoe handles that.

While you're there, you should make an appointment with the nutritionist.''

"Okay."

He glanced up sharply. Her agreement was too casual, too ready to be true. He bet she had no intention of following a nutritionist's regime, even supposing she kept the appointment. "I'm serious, Ms. Hanson," he said, writing her referral. "Your job isn't conducive to a healthy lifestyle, as amply shown by your collapse. From what I've heard, models play hard—''

"And *work* hard," she protested.

He tried to keep the skepticism out of his expression. "The point is, you need to take care of yourself."

"Doctor…" She hesitated before going on. "Have you ever had a patient who's died and come back? Someone who had a near-death experience?"

"No, I haven't." He tore the referral note from the pad, folded it and put it in an envelope. "But I know that near-death experiences are hallucinations brought on by a lack of oxygen to the brain when the heart stops pumping blood."

"You *know* that, do you?" she said, her face troubled.

"It's the accepted medical explanation. Why? Do you think you had a near-death experience?"

"Yes, and it was no hallucination," she said earnestly. "When I was in the hospital in Milan someone brought in an English newspaper. In it was an article about a Dutch study that monitored the vital signs of patients who reported near-death experiences. One man even described the doctors removing his dentures before putting a tube down his throat to revive him. All this while he had no pulse and no detectable brain activity. What do you think of that?"

"Unconvincing. I read the original article written up in the British medical journal *Lancet*. There're plenty of other studies that prove the experiences are generated by the brain as it faces the trauma of death. In my opinion the Dutch study doesn't prove there's life after death."

"But I met my m—" She broke off abruptly and, to Ben's relief, waved away the topic of conversation. "Never mind." Then she noticed the framed photo on his desk of him and Eddie standing on the stone steps of a ruined Mayan temple. "That must be your brother. He's a doctor, too, isn't he?"

"Yes." He handed her the referral envelope. "How did you know?"

Geena Hanson grinned, and the sophisticated model turned into a mischievous girl. "This is a small town. By the end of the week I'll know your brand of toothpaste.''

Her grin charmed him even more than her beauty, but he was careful not to let it show. ''Be sure to see the nutritionist. And I'd like to see you again in a couple months for a follow-up examination.''

She lingered in the doorway, her gaze roving over him. ''What brings you to Hainesville, Doctor?''

He found himself standing closer to her than necessary, drinking in the blue of her eyes while her perfume continued to befuddle his senses. Her smile invited flirtation, and he lost the struggle to maintain a strictly professional manner. ''When you find out,'' he drawled, ''let me know.''

She laughed, a spontaneous guffaw at odds with her elegance. ''I'll do that,'' she said, and glided away.

''Next,'' Ben called. But the waiting room had filled while he'd been seeing Geena, and the patients didn't know any better than he did whose turn it was. The batch of mixed-up files was no help. A mother with a crying child, an elderly man, a teenage boy in a cast and a middle-aged woman stared blankly at him. Then they all began talking at once, claiming priority.

Geena paused at the exit, one hand on the doorknob, and studied the situation. Ben Matthews, competent doctor though he was, was clearly out of his depth. Her first instinct was to go to his assistance. But, she argued with herself, she knew nothing about being a receptionist in a medical clinic. The old Geena would have walked; the new Geena saw a person in need. The woman in her mentally hugged herself. For a while longer she would enjoy the company of this delicious man with the intelligent eyes and the air of adventure still clinging to his woven shirt.

She strode to the reception desk and picked up the stack of patient files before scanning the room. She'd never done this sort of work before, but how hard could it be? She knew most of the folks here. Add a little common sense and a lot of compassion...

The little girl crying and twisting in her mother's lap while she clutched at her ear was clearly in pain.

"Laura," Geena called, recognizing the mom as one of Erin's high school friends. "You go next."

"Thanks. She's got an ear infection." With obvious relief, Laura carried her sick daughter past Ben into the examining room.

Geena felt a hand on her arm, and Ben pulled her to one side. "What do you think you're doing?"

Calmly disregarding his annoyed tone, she said, "I expect your patients could use some help organizing themselves. Not everyone is as enterprising as I am.''

''Indeed.'' Beneath his mustache, his compressed lips curved a little. Then he glanced at the waiting room, where his patients had settled back to their magazines with resigned acceptance. Eyebrows raised, Ben shrugged. ''Okay.''

Geena seated herself at the reception desk and began to arrange the files in the order in which she thought best. When Laura and her little girl were through, she helped Mr. Marshall to his feet, then handed the elderly gentleman his cane.

Ben paused beside the reception desk to pick up Mr. Marshall's file. ''I take it you're staying awhile?''

''I don't know,'' she said, pretending to consider the matter. ''I've got a lot to do today.'' Touch up her nail polish, read the latest issue of *Vogue,* yawn a couple of dozen times from boredom. She'd barely been home a week and already she was going crazy. ''But since you asked so nicely...all right.''

She leaned across the desk and added in an undertone, ''Mr. Marshall has gout in his big toe, has had for years. But he's sensitive about his feet. Be nice.''

One side of his mouth curled up. ''I'm always nice.''

Geena was sure he was, in spite of his lack of understanding about near-death experiences. Certainly, he wasn't like other men she knew, European playboys and New York stockbrokers, men with no one's interests at heart but their own. Despite his obvious disapproval of *her,* Ben Matthews struck her as a very caring man. And an attractive one. While he'd been reading her file, she'd studied him. She liked his tall, solid body and his wry smile. She liked his long tapered fingers that held a fountain pen instead of an ordinary ballpoint. She liked the slight wave in his dark hair and the faint color that had appeared in his cheeks when he'd listened to her heart. But it was his Texas drawl that made her insides weak.

Ben escorted Mr. Marshall to the examining room, and Geena tackled the accumulated fliers from medical supply and pharmaceutical companies cluttering the desk, finding unexpected satisfaction in putting the office in order. The outside door opened, and she turned to see who had come in.

"Geena Hanson, is that you?" the woman shrieked.

Geena let out a yell. "Linda Thirsk! I can't believe it. I haven't seen you in years." She hurried around the desk to hug her high school friend.

Laughing, the two women stepped apart to look at

each other. "You're so skinny I hate you," Linda said. Linda had become comfortably plump over the years, but somehow the extra pounds suited her, and her buttercup yellow dress was a flattering cut.

"You look great," Geena declared. "So, did you ever make it to Greenwich Village to write satirical novels?"

Linda laughed. "I got as far as Spokane before my car broke down. Toby O'Conner heard about it from my mom and drove his tow truck all the way out to get me. We've been together ever since. Three kids, all under eight."

"Lucky you. What about your writing?"

Linda gave her an odd, sly smile. "Oh, I do the church newsletter and other bits and pieces. Hey, we're having our tenth high school reunion in October. You've got to come."

Geena's smile faded, and her cheeks burned with embarrassment. "I...I don't know if I can. Don't you remember? I left high school after grade eleven to take a modeling contract. How can I go to the reunion when I never graduated?"

"No one will care about that," Linda insisted. "You've got to come."

Easy for Linda to say. She'd been top of their class, and despite their friendship, Geena had always felt slightly intimidated by her brainpower, even if

Linda hadn't made it to New York. "I'll have to let you know."

Geena went to the desk. "Did you have an appointment?"

"For two o'clock. Are you working here?"

"Just for today. The receptionist is away, and Dr. Matthews hasn't got a new one yet." Geena glanced from right to left, then whispered, "I'm having so much fun playing receptionist—you have no idea. But things are a little disorganized. You might have to wait a few minutes."

"That's okay." Linda lifted a laptop computer. "I'll just take a seat and get caught up on my, uh, newsletter."

"Talk to you later."

The examining room door opened and out came a man in his late forties with unnaturally black hair and a pale-blue suit jacket over his arm. Geena recognized Ray Ronstadt, Kelly's real estate boss. According to Kelly, he was newly divorced and on the prowl.

"Thanks, Doc," Ray said, rolling down his sleeve. "When will you have the results?"

"Wednesday morning. Give me a call." Ben cast a questioning glance at Geena. "Next?"

"Mrs. Chan." She reached for the chart and with a nod indicated an elderly patient. Before Geena could hand the chart to Ben, Ray swaggered to the desk.

"Hey, Geena," he said, buttoning his cuff with a nearsighted squint. "Kelly told me you were back in town. If you get bored with this one-horse burg you can always take a ride on the wild side with yours truly."

Ben, still waiting for the chart and for Mrs. Chan to shuffle across the waiting room, frowned.

"Gosh, Ray, that sounds like too much excitement for me," she said, smiling blandly. "Dr. Matthews says I've got to take it easy after my collapse."

Ray appeared taken aback. "Oh, yeah. Sorry to hear about that." He stuck out his neck as he adjusted his tie. "You look damn fine to me."

"That's very kind." She tilted her head to one side, pen poised. "Did you need another appointment?"

"Nah. I'll call for the results of my blood test in a few days." He smoothed his hair with both hands. "A single guy who gets a bit of action has to be careful these days. It's the least I can do for my lady friends."

"How thoughtful of you." *Gross!* Geena heard Linda's suppressed giggle and was careful not to catch her eye.

"So how about dinner?" Ray went on undeterred.

"The steak house in Simcoe has a two-for-one deal on Tuesdays."

"Uh, thanks, Ray, but I'm really busy on Tuesday." She rose and walked toward the exit.

He followed like a lamb. "I guess a gal like you gets lots of invitations."

"Hundreds. Thousands. More than I can accommodate." She opened the door and ushered him through. "Bye now."

Geena handed Ben the chart just as Mrs. Chan made it to the examining room doorway.

"Very smooth," Ben murmured to Geena. "Maybe we should get another appointment book for all your invitations. Maybe your own secretary."

She slanted him a glance. "I don't need a book to remember the invitations I *accept*."

To her disappointment, he didn't take the hint. Just escorted Mrs. Chan into the examining room. Geena shrugged and returned to the desk.

Late in the afternoon, long after Linda had seen the doctor and left, the door opened, and a woman came in with a baby in her arms and a young boy by the hand. The woman's long, dark hair was pulled into a straggly ponytail, and she wore a beaded muslin blouse, which Geena recognized as vintage 1960s, over a long flowing skirt.

"Hi, I'm Carrie Wakefield," she said. "My son,

Tod, has an appointment.'' She pushed the boy forward and shifted a runny-nosed baby to her other hip. "Sorry we're late.''

"That's okay." Geena looked at the boy, who had a cowlick and was wearing striped pants and cowboy boots. "Hi, Tod."

Tod regarded her solemnly out of round brown eyes. His face was thin and too pale for a boy off school for the summer. "When a pig is sick, what kind of medicine do you use?"

Geena frowned. Did the boy mistake this for a veterinary clinic? "Gosh, Tod, I don't know. What's wrong with the pig?"

His face crinkled in an impish grin. "You use *oinkment!* Get it?"

Geena laughed. "That's cute. How old are you, Tod?"

"Nine and a quarter. Why don't hippos play basketball?"

"Um…they're not tall enough?"

"They don't look good in shorts." Tod gave a deprecating shrug. "That one's not very good—hippos don't even wear shorts." Then he informed her, "I've got monster glue at home."

"Come and sit down, Tod, and don't bother the lady." Carrie Wakefield looked worn-out and out of patience as she jiggled her crying baby in her arms.

"I'm not bothering her." Tod turned to Geena. "Am I?"

"Not at all." Geena rose from the desk. "Come with me, Tod." She led him to a small table in a corner of the waiting room with toys and books for children. "Do you want to play with the trucks?"

"I want you to read to me." He shoved his hands in his pants pockets.

"Tod," his weary mother remonstrated. To Geena, she said, "He's going into grade four and is perfectly capable of reading for himself."

"That's okay." Geena studied the boy. His expression was half defiant, half needy, as if he was starved for attention and used to getting short-changed. She wondered what was wrong with him besides having a baby brother who required a lot of his mother's time.

"I'd love to read to you, Tod. How about this one," she said, showing him a collection of Calvin and Hobbes cartoons.

Tod's face lit. "I wish I had a pet tiger."

"Me, too." She patted the bench beside her.

Tod leaned unselfconsciously against her side, and she was agreeably aware of his small body snuggling up to her. *This is what having a child would feel like,* she thought as she opened the book. Ten minutes later they were giggling at Calvin's outrageous antics when she sensed someone watching them. Geena looked up to see Ben in the doorway, his dark eyes thoughtful.

"It's time for you to see the doctor," she said, closing the book.

"We haven't finished," Tod protested.

"Come, Tod." Carrie rose, her baby asleep in her arms.

When they'd all trooped into the examining room, Geena tidied the magazines and toys in the waiting room. Tod was Ben's last patient, and though she was tired, she also acknowledged that this was the most satisfying day she'd had all week. She'd enjoyed playing with the children and reminiscing with the elderly. What was she going to do tomorrow?

Maybe, she thought, as she watered the potted plants, Ben would decide she'd done such a wonderful job today he would hire her. The tasks were so different from what she was used to and so relatively stress-free that working here would seem like a holiday. As a bonus, she'd get to know Ben Matthews.

And if he got to know her, he'd see she wasn't the irresponsible, self-indulgent person he obviously considered her to be. Okay, maybe she *used* to be that way, but she'd been given a new slate, so to speak, to write on as she would. All she had to do was figure out who she was and what she wanted to do with her life.

She was gazing out the window of the empty waiting room, watering can forgotten in her hands, when Tod and his mother emerged. Carrie Wakefield's face looked pinched and white, and Tod was very quiet.

"Bye, Tod." Geena put down the watering can and walked them to the door, holding it open as the little family filed through. "Bye, Carrie."

She watched them from the window as they climbed into a battered Honda Civic and drove away.

Ben came and stood behind her. "Tod has acute lymphocytic leukemia."

"Oh, no." Geena made a soft sound of remorse in her throat. "That sweet little boy. How bad is it? Is it treatable?"

"Pretty bad, but yes, it's treatable. He's going into the hospital for chemotherapy tomorrow." Ben sounded detached, but Geena could see in his eyes that he was deeply distressed. "He was diagnosed early. With treatment, he'll be fine. Just fine."

She wanted to believe him. She *did* believe him.

"You were a big help today," he said, turning to her. "An amazing help. Thank you."

Geena shrugged, ridiculously pleased at his praise. Would her little fantasy come true? "I enjoyed it. In fact, I could come in again tomorrow if you want me to.''

''Ah.'' Ben grimaced. ''I appreciate your offer, but I'm after a qualified RN to act as a nurse receptionist. With such a small practice I need someone who can take blood samples, tend to small wounds, that sort of thing.''

''Oh, of course.'' Blood rushed to her cheeks. What was she thinking? Of course he'd want someone qualified. Not *her,* whose only talent was looking beautiful.

''I'll pay you for today, of course,'' he said quickly.

As if this was about money. She gave him a brilliant smile. ''Absolutely not necessary. As I said, I enjoyed it.''

Moving past him, she returned the watering can to the kitchenette and got her purse out of the desk drawer.

''Don't forget to get those blood samples taken and make an appointment with the nutritionist,'' he said.

''I won't.'' She paused at the exit to give him a cheery wave and another smile. ''Ciao.''

She kept her head high until she was around the corner from the clinic, then, despite all her training in deportment, she couldn't help but let her shoulders slump.

That she'd saved enough to enjoy a wealthy life-style for the rest of her life, even if she never worked again, made no difference. That hundreds of men at one time or another had vied for her attention made no difference. Ben Matthews wasn't impressed by beauty or money or fame.

And face it, if you took away those things, what did she have? Nothing.

Deep inside, she knew she *was* somebody, but no one besides her family ever bothered to look past the surface to see the real her. Especially not intelligent, educated men like Ben.

CHAPTER THREE

"HAVE ANOTHER chocolate doughnut," Edna said, pushing the plate toward Ben.

Edna Thompson, the elderly woman who owned the bed and breakfast where Ben was staying until his rental house became available, had coffee and doughnuts waiting for him every day when he got back from work. She loved to talk about her health, or lack of it.

"Did I mention I have a pain here, in my left hip?" She slapped the bony buttock beneath her floral cotton shift, just in case Ben had missed that anatomy lesson. "What do you suppose it is?"

"Possibly referred pain from your lower spine," Ben said around a mouthful of doughnut. "Come into the clinic tomorrow, and I'll check it out."

"Maybe I will. It's a pity you're moving next week. Having a doctor in the house is nice—kind of like having my own personal physician." Edna got up from the table and went to the fridge.

Ben reached for the copy of the *Hainesville Herald*

Edna had left on the table and skimmed the headlines. Hot debate raged over whether the town needed a traffic light at the corner of Main and Dakota.

"I heard Geena Hanson was helping you out in the clinic today," Edna said, busily placing frozen sausage rolls from a commercial package onto a foil-lined baking tray. "That girl is skin and bones. Ruth—that's her grandmother and my best friend—tells me she just pushes her food around her plate. Can't you do anything for her?"

"I'm trying. She needs to recognize she has a problem before she can fix it."

He was still puzzled by Geena's disappointment—which all the smiles in the world couldn't hide—at not being given a job at the clinic. Although probably she found life in Hainesville slow and simple after the jet-set scene. The town was a culture shock to him, too, but for the opposite reason. Paved streets, abundant consumer goods…heck, even electricity in every home was a big step up from where he'd been. People in small towns were pretty much the same the world over, though, friendly, a little nosy, but always willing to help their neighbor.

Edna shook her white head. "It's not healthy for anyone to be that thin. Did I mention I had another gall bladder attack?"

"Maybe you should have it out."

Edna glanced up. "You think so?"

"I could do it right now, if you like," Ben suggested, straight-faced. "I used to operate in far more primitive circumstances in Guatemala. I'll just go get my bag with my scalpel."

Edna jerked back. "No way are you cutting me open on my kitchen table—" She broke into laughter as his mouth began to twitch. "You wicked boy!"

"Sorry, Edna," he said, chuckling along with her. He rose and put his arm around her shoulder. "How about letting me buy you dinner at the Burger Shack tonight?"

Every Friday night he treated himself to a Humungoburger, onion rings and chocolate milk shake. A *large* chocolate milk shake. A dinner like that was probably murder on his cholesterol count, but what the heck, that was why he jogged.

"Why, thank you, Ben. But Friday night is my regular bridge night with the girls. We all bring a little something to snack on while we play." She crumpled the sausage roll package and threw it in the trash. "Say, you won't tell anyone these aren't homemade, will you?"

"My lips are sealed." Who would he tell? Although he liked the town and its people well enough, he hadn't yet made friends.

"The other gals are good cooks, but me—I don't have the knack. I tell them the sausage rolls are my grandmother's recipe." She grinned evilly. "But I buy them in Simcoe."

Outside, a car horn beeped. "That'll be Martha," Edna said. "She's still got her license."

Edna took up her cane, but before she could reach for the tray of sausage rolls Ben said, "Allow me," and carried them to Martha's car. The early-model Volvo was in pristine condition. Ben speculated that Martha had been driving it since it rolled off the production line in 1958.

After Edna and Martha drove off, Ben sat in the wooden deck chair on the porch, savoring the balmy evening and the sweet scent of virburnum growing in big pots by the steps. The light hadn't yet begun to fade and children were playing scrub baseball in the vacant lot down the street. An older couple out for an evening stroll waved to him from across the street. Ben waved back and realized suddenly what he liked so much about Hainesville. It was roughly the same size as the small Texas town he'd grown up in.

The phone in the kitchen rang, and he went inside to answer it. "Hello?"

"Ben?"

Through the static, Ben recognized his brother's

voice. "Eddie! I was wondering when you'd find a moment to call. How's it going there? Are you finding your way around?"

"Everything's fine," Eddie said. "Except for the rain. It's been pouring for days now."

"Did I neglect to mention the rainy season?"

"Mostly it's interesting," Eddie went on in a lighter tone. "Today I was given a live chicken in lieu of payment. The fool thing is pecking apart my kitchen as we speak."

Picturing it, Ben laughed. "You're supposed to *eat* the bird, not keep it as a pet."

"I was afraid of that, but I can't bring myself to wring the poor thing's neck. How is Hainesville? Are you enjoying being back in civilization?"

Ben took the cordless phone and went outside. "Hainesville is a treat. It's got one stoplight, a mayor who goes fishing with the bank manager in the middle of the workday and the best hamburgers in the country. Right now I'm sitting on the front porch, breathing in the summer evening and watching the world stroll by."

"Sounds idyllic. I can almost hear you slapping the paint on your white picket fence. Found yourself a wife yet?"

"Give me a day or two, would you? Oh, you'll never guess…remember that model who collapsed in

Milan, the one whose picture was in the newspaper you brought the day you arrived? She's here. She grew up in Hainesville and has come home to recuperate.''

"And you're her GP." Eddie laughed. "Just deserts, big brother, just deserts."

"Oh, she's dessert, all right. But man cannot live on cake and ice cream alone." Then he felt bad joking about Geena. She *had* helped him out. "Actually, she's okay."

"If you like that sort of thing," Eddie said dryly.

"Which I don't." Sure, he found her attractive in a glamorous, superficial sort of way, but the idea of him getting involved with her was laughable. Geena Hanson was about as much his type as prissy Greta Vogler.

"Are you taking your malaria pills?" he said, as much to change the subject as because he couldn't help looking after his little brother.

"Yes, *Mom*. Oh, hey, I'd better go. A couple of teachers from the next village are meeting me at the cantina."

As Eddie spoke, Ben could almost hear the sound of marimba music, and he experienced a pang of homesickness for the village. "Have a *cerveza* for me, bro. And keep in touch."

"Will do. How about we make this a regular time for me to call every week?"

"Sounds like a plan. I'll give you my number at the clinic, too, in case I'm working late." He recited the phone number to Eddie, then signed off. "Talk to you next week, little buddy."

THE NEXT DAY the heat woke Geena early. When she saw it was ten a.m. she kicked off the ivory damask bedspread, leaving her naked body covered only by an Egyptian cotton sheet, and snuggled deeper into the mound of rose-patterned pillows. With no reason to get up, she let her imagination flow in a fantasy of herself and Ben Matthews in a delicious, if implausible, scenario involving a stethoscope and an examining bed.

At noon, she dragged herself out of bed, dressed in a simple linen sheath and dabbed on perfume from a crystal bottle. Then she wandered down to the kitchen, wondering what she was going to do with herself for the next few months. Picking an apple out of the fruit bowl, she put her nose to the rosy skin and inhaled the sweet-tart scent. Reluctantly, she put the fruit in the bowl. She was hungry, but then, she was always hungry. Denying herself food had become a habit.

Steps sounded on the back porch, and Gran came

in, breathing heavily and wiping perspiration from her brow. "Man, is it hot out there. But I had a heck of a workout," she panted. "I met Marvin Taylor outside the Knit 'n Kneedles and we racewalked all the way up Linden Street."

"Are you sure you're not overdoing it, Gran?" Geena asked, noting the damp patches on her grandmother's sweatshirt. Since recovering from her minor heart attack a year ago, Gran was taking her exercise very seriously.

"I'm in training for the seniors' fun run," Gran said. "Of course, at my age, run is a misnomer, and it stops being fun after the first mile. But we're raising money for a new maternity wing on the Hainesville Hospital. Greta Vogler just won't let that project go. The woman's like a bull terrier."

Greta Vogler. The woman who had branded her father a drunk driver, tarnishing his memory and Geena and her sisters' lives growing up. Geena went to the fridge for a bottle of mineral water. "Does Miss Vogler still teach at the high school?"

Gran balanced a hand on the kitchen countertop and stretched her quads. "She's vice principal now. Which reminds me—Linda Thirsk called. She wants to know if you've decided about your high school reunion."

Geena shrugged and sipped her water. "I can't believe she married Tubby O'Conner."

Gran moved on to her hamstrings. "Linda's phone number is on the pad on the counter. She's probably home now. Why not give her a call?" When Geena made no move to pick up the phone, Gran stopped stretching. "You *are* going, aren't you?"

Geena drained her bottle and put it beside the sink. The high school reunion, Ben... Everything conspired to remind her of her deficiencies.

"How can I?" she said, and was dismayed to hear her voice waver. "I never graduated."

"Does it matter? You've become such a big success." Behind her large-framed plastic glasses, Gran's eyes showed regret, sympathy and a trace of guilt, none of which eased Geena's self-doubt.

"Such a success I nearly killed myself. I'm going for a walk," she said. "I'll see you later." With no idea where she was headed, she took off down the hall and out the front door.

"Geena," Gran called after her. "Will you be back for lunch?"

"I'm not hungry."

Geena's restless footsteps carried her into town on sidewalks shimmering with the late-summer heat. Past Blackwell's Drugstore, past the bank where Erin had been assistant manager until she had the baby, past Orville's Barber Shop...

She hadn't spoken to Orville since she'd been back and she knew he'd like her to drop in. A close friend of her father's, he'd been like a favorite uncle while she'd been growing up. She peered in the barbershop window. Orville had his back to her, busy cutting someone's hair.

The bell above the door sounded as she pushed through to the cool interior that held the familiar mingled scents of Old Spice and hair products. "Hi, Orville."

Orville, a dapper man in his fifties, was dressed as always in neatly pressed slacks and a cashmere sweater. At the sound of her voice he turned with a wide smile and came forward to greet her. "Geena! How's my best girl?"

"If I'm your best girl, who do you take out on Saturday night?" she teased. Geena had always thought it a waste that Orville, who had been widowed young, had never remarried. "I'm fine. How are you?"

"Same as usual," he said good-naturedly. "One step behind the tax man, one step ahead of the Grim Reaper."

Then he moved to one side, and through the mirror Geena glimpsed the face of the man in the chair. *Ben*.

Surprise and pleasure tinged with embarrassment flowed through her. Embarrassment because it wasn't every day a man turned her down—for *any* reason.

Orville returned to his work with a flourish of comb and scissors. Geena sauntered to the counter and perched on the edge, facing Ben. The only way to get over embarrassment was to meet it head-on. "Hi, there."

"Hi, yourself." His warm gaze traveled over her. "All of Hainesville is wilting in the heat, and yet you manage to look like the proverbial cucumber."

"It's an illusion, cultivated by years spent in front of klieg lights," Geena said lightly. She turned to the barber. "So, Orville, what hair magic are you working on the doctor? A quiff? A coif?"

"Just a trim," Orville said, snipping carefully around Ben's ears. "Right, Doc?"

Ben nodded. Geena wriggled farther onto the counter. "Orville used to cut my hair, too."

"Until at the very grown-up age of six you decided you required a stylist and made your grandmother take you to the beauty salon in Simcoe," Orville elaborated.

"That was before Wendy opened up shop here." Geena eyed Ben, her head tilted to one side. "With that goatee and mustache, and draped in that black hairdresser's cape, you look a little like Zorro."

Ben's right eyebrow rose, giving him a wicked, humorous expression. "You like, *señorita?*"

"It's rather nineties," she teased, meaning the goatee. "But I guess you can get away with it in Hainesville."

"Are you suggesting this isn't the fashion capital of the Pacific northwest?" Orville demanded, reaching for hair gel. "That everything's not up-to-date in Kansas City?"

"Hainesville isn't on the fashion map," Ben replied for her. "I daresay it's not even on the same planet as Paris or Milan." He held up a copy of the magazine in his lap, which, to Geena's surprise, turned out to be *Vogue*—with her photo on the cover. "As you can see, I'm studying up on the matter."

Geena glanced down—and saw a two-page spread of herself at a New York fashion show three seasons ago. "Ugh. I was so fat back then. Orville, what are you doing with *Vogue* in your waiting room? You used to have nothing but *Rod and Gun* and *Readers' Digest.*"

"Kelly dropped them off—she said she was distributing her old copies around town rather than throwing them away. You'd be surprised how many men pick them up."

The bell over the door sounded, and a man Geena didn't know came in. Orville excused himself and went to the desk to make the newcomer an appointment.

Ben continued to peruse the photos of Geena. "The extra weight looked good on you."

"I was hideous. Flip the page." She began arranging Orville's brushes and combs, spreading them out in a fan on the counter. She didn't know what was worse—Ben seeing her that way or Ben admiring her that way.

Ben's voice was quiet but penetrating. "You're beautiful, Geena. Why you don't like yourself?"

A jolt ran through her. Her gaze jerked up to meet his in the mirror. *"What are you talking about? Of course I like myself."* Then she realized she was being too intense and shrugged, adding lightly, "After that show some young thang from Georgia took over top billing. I had to do something to get my mojo back."

Ben said nothing, just slowly shook his head. The silence worked on her, conjuring conflicting voices.

People told her she was beautiful all the time. It meant nothing.

He wouldn't say it if he didn't mean it.

Ben was a doctor, concerned about the health effects of low body weight.

Why should she care what he thought?

Orville came back, and Geena hopped down from

the counter with a brilliant smile and kissed him on both cheeks. "I've got to go. Ciao." Making it seem almost an afterthought, Geena waggled her fingers over her shoulder. "Bye, Ben."

"She was in a hurry all of a sudden," Orville said as the door shut behind her. He shrugged and picked up the hand mirror to show Ben the cut from all angles. "What do you think? Is it short enough or do you want some more off?"

"The hair's fine." Ben stroked his chin and twisted his face from side to side as he gazed at his reflection. Too nineties, huh? What was wrong with the nineties? And why should he give her opinion so much credence?

GEENA WALKED two doors down and entered the coffee shop. She ordered a skinny cappuccino and sat where she could see the front window—in case Ben walked by. She wasn't sure if she did that because she wanted him to join her or so she could avoid him if she saw him first. Boy, did that guy get under her skin. It was only a matter of time before he asked her out. She would have to invent some excuse, of course—she couldn't possibly accept the first invitation, or one given on short notice—but she could subtly let him know he had her permission to ask her out again.

JOAN KILBY   75

Geena lingered until her coffee was nothing but dried froth on the inside of the cup and the smell of bacon frying on the grill drove her crazy with hunger. Finally she had to acknowledge that Ben wasn't going to walk by, or join her for coffee, or ask her out—today.

With a sigh, she paid for her order and went out. She crossed the road, turned off the main road and aimlessly wandered the residential streets, renewing her acquaintance with Hainesville.

Before she knew it, she was standing in front of Hainesville High. The two-story brick building was closed for the summer, and the empty playing fields and shuttered windows gave it a somnolent look. If only she'd graduated. Maybe it wasn't too late to finish high school. She tried to picture herself, at age twenty-nine, sitting in a row of desks with pimply-faced boys and giggling girls.

No way, she decided with a shudder.

When she'd been a little girl, she'd dreamed of an important career—doctor, lawyer, physicist. Then she'd started to blossom, and suddenly no one noticed anything about her but her beauty.

She'd been glad enough to leave school at the age of sixteen; now, though, she realized she'd missed a normal young adulthood. She'd partied hard, traveled constantly and hadn't used her brain for much more than calculating the time difference between New York and Paris. Oh, she had street smarts and she'd picked up survival strategies young; she'd had to, to be successful. But essays, calculus, science—those seemed too much for a weak and lazy mind.

There were many things she adored about being a model—beautiful clothes, foreign travel, celebrity parties. And it wasn't as though her brain was *entirely* empty. She knew the hottest nightclubs in every capital city in the world. She knew who was doing who and who was suing who. She knew how to make a designer's creations sing and how to glide down a runway like the queen of the universe.

And yet...something was missing. Ever since her near-death experience, she'd been aware of a lack of substance in her life. She wanted to be taken seriously, to be listened to. Geena sighed. She rarely expressed an opinion because she was ill-informed. She knew who the President was but not how the electoral college system worked. She knew John Steinbeck was a great author but had no idea what his contribution to American literature was. She knew the sky was blue but couldn't say why. There was so much knowledge in the world, and she had a handle on practically none of it.

She wanted to do something meaningful with her

life. Something that would help others. Maybe education was the key to a different future—

A noise behind her made her turn. Greta Vogler was sweeping her front path, one birdlike gray eye on Geena. She'd forgotten that her ex-teacher lived across from the school, had for thirty-odd years. Greta was the perennial old maid, buttoned up to her sharp chin in bulky cardigans and midcalf skirts two decades out of date.

Geena might have felt sorry for Greta if seeing her hadn't brought a flood of negative emotions for the woman who'd spread malicious rumors about her dead parents. Geena wanted to walk away, but she remembered her mother's gentle suggestion that she forgive Greta. Geena couldn't quite find it in her heart to be that saintlike, but she managed to call a polite greeting.

Greta took that as an invitation to cross the road, broom in hand. ''Hello, my dear. How nice to have you back in town. I was very sorry to hear about your collapse.'' She eyed Geena up and down. ''No wonder, though, when you're nothing but skin and bones.''

Geena was *very* tired of hearing about her weight. ''Miss Vogler, I was wondering, can a person do high school by correspondence?''

''Ah, that's right, you never finished grade

twelve." Greta nodded sagely. "I always thought Ruth was remiss in allowing you to go away so young."

Geena shrugged. "Education is probably wasted on a dummy like me, anyway."

Greta looked at her sharply. "Why do you talk like that? Anyone would think you were doing it merely to be contradicted. Isn't it enough that you're rich and famous?"

Taken aback, Geena stared. Why *did* she talk like that? She didn't really believe it—she just thought everyone else did. "You're right. I'm sorry."

"No need to apologize, either. But if you want to continue your education, why don't you get your graduate equivalent diploma?"

Geena glanced around, making sure no one was there to overhear. This was embarrassing enough just between her and Greta. "What is that? I don't think I could attend class."

Greta clutched her broom to her bosom. "The GED is equivalent to a high school diploma in that it allows you college entry. You don't need to go to classes to sit the exam."

"That sounds pretty good." With her GED she could hold her head up at the high school reunion. Who knows, maybe she would go on to college. But good grief, she was entrusting her secret to the biggest gossip in Hainesville. She would hate it if people found out, especially Ben. Really, she didn't care what he thought of her body, if only he admired her mind.

"I'm interested, but please, Miss Vogler, it's very important to me that we keep this between ourselves. And I have a time constraint—the third week in September."

"Ah, your tenth reunion. I suppose you would be embarrassed for your friends to be reminded that in spite of your worldly success, you still don't have the basic building blocks of education."

Geena forced her mouth into a frozen smile. "You always explain things so clearly."

"That's what makes me a good teacher." Greta swept a twig off the sidewalk and into the gutter. "I can help you, but you'll have to work hard. Don't think you can slack off the way you did when you were sixteen. Your beauty won't carry you forever. It's a good thing you found that out sooner rather than later."

Geena could taste blood where she was biting her tongue. "I'll do whatever it takes."

Greta's black eyes gleamed. "I'm glad you feel that way, because I was hoping you would do me a little favor in return. I've been meaning to come and talk to you about it in any case."

"I'd be happy to help," Geena heard herself promise.

"You probably know I'm trying to raise money for a maternity wing on the hospital," Greta went on. "The ladies' auxiliary is holding a bingo night and will donate the proceeds to the maternity wing fund. I'd like you to put on one of your fancy dresses and call out the numbers."

A bingo announcer. Geena didn't know whether to laugh or cry. "I'm not too good with numbers, Greta." She thought fast. "But speaking of fancy dresses, I have another idea. How about a fashion show?"

Greta frowned and swept an ant off the path in front of her. "I don't know anything about fashion."

"I do. It'll be great. We'll advertise all over the county and raise a ton of money."

At the prospect of a big return, Greta's frown lifted, but she warned, "You'd have to convince the ladies' auxiliary. They have their hearts set on a bingo night. Come along to our next meeting, and we'll talk about it."

CHAPTER FOUR

BEN UNCAPPED his pen and wrote out a prescription for Mrs. Gribble. The fingers of his other hand idly rubbed his smooth upper lip, and the gesture brought to mind his last encounter with Geena. At his elbow, the stack of lab reports—rather, the *absence* of a certain set of blood tests—also reminded him of Geena. As for the photos of her in *Vogue*—they were etched on his cerebral cortex.

Stifling a yawn behind his hand, he struggled to keep his writing legible. It had been a long day, and he was tired. He'd spent the wee hours of the morning pondering the ethics of dating a patient. A patient unsuited to him in every way, with a high profile in a small town. A patient who hid a deep vulnerability beneath her bravado. He bet she fooled most people, but she didn't fool him. Unfortunately, it made him like her more rather than less.

His new nurse receptionist, Barbara, was highly qualified and extremely efficient. But she didn't have the rapport with his patients Geena had, nor did she brighten the clinic with warmth and laughter the way Geena did. If it wasn't such an unthinkably stupid idea, he'd have been tempted to hire Geena back just to have her around.

"There you go, Geena," he murmured, and passed the prescription across the desk.

Mabel Gribble, waiting patiently and plumply, arms folded across her substantial lap, chuckled. "I think your mind has wandered, Doctor. I'm Mabel."

Aghast, Ben glanced up to see Mabel regarding him with good-natured inquisitiveness. "Er, sorry, I was thinking of something else."

"Don't you mean *someone?*" Mabel asked coyly. "I take it you were referring to Geena Hanson? She's absolutely lovely, isn't she? Like a young Audrey Hepburn." Mabel sighed. "I wish I had her figure."

"No, you don't, not really." Ben rose, signaling her visit was over. "Take three of those tablets a day, with meals, and your stomach pain should improve quickly."

Ben saw Mrs. Gribble out and ushered in his next patient, a young woman whose neat, rounded figure was displayed to advantage in snug-fitting jeans and a scoop-necked T-shirt. "Ms. Morrissy, is it? Was that you I saw shepherding preschoolers past the clinic the other day?"

She brushed back a swathe of thick dark hair, coloring slightly as if pleased he'd recognized her. "Please, call me Tricia. I run the day care. I was taking the kids to the park. Oh, and by the way, it's *miss.*"

Ben assumed a friendly but bland expression at the emphasis on her single status. Tricia Morrissy wasn't the first woman in Hainesville to come on to him; as a young, unattached doctor he supposed he was a prime target. "So, Tricia. What seems to be the matter?"

"I twisted my back picking up one of the children, and now it's so sore I can hardly move." She arched her back, digging a fist into her lower spine. Her upthrust breasts, molded by the knit fabric, were lovely. Ben's glance, though, held nothing but professional detachment.

"Stand up and we'll test your range of movement."

He stood behind her and moved her arms, then got her to twist her spine and bend over, prodding with his fingers to locate the source of the pain as he questioned her about the injury.

"I understand you're not married," Tricia said when he'd garnered the information he needed about her back. "Have you made many friends in Hainesville?"

"I'm slowly getting to know people," he replied

cautiously. He had an idea what was coming and wished he could avoid turning her down. At the same time, a voice in his head was saying, *Idiot. Why not go out with her?*

"A group of us go dancing in Simcoe every Friday." Tricia turned and smiled at him, blushing a little. "I could use a partner if you're available."

She was pretty, single and sweet. But not only didn't she light his fire, she didn't produce so much as a spark. In other words, *she wasn't Geena.* "I, uh, appreciate the offer, but I have a standing engagement on Friday nights."

"Oh, well," she said with a shrug and a smile, "you can't blame a girl for trying."

"No, indeed. Now, about your back... You've strained some muscles, but there doesn't appear to be any damage to the ligaments or joints," he said, writing a prescription. "Back problems usually fix themselves with time. Walking is good. The anti-inflammatories I'd like you to take will help with the pain."

"Thanks, Doctor," she said, accepting the slip of paper. "If you change your mind about Friday night, you know where to find me."

"I'll remember that. Should you get any numbness or tingling in your back or legs, come and see me right away. And make sure you bend your knees when you lift those kids.''

When she'd left, he told Barbara to hold the next patient while he made a phone call. Then he got out Geena's file and dialed her number, reminding himself that he was *not* happy with her and he should *not* sound too pleased when she answered.

GEENA SLAMMED SHUT the math textbook Greta had loaned her and pushed away from her old student desk, stretching her cramped legs. She hadn't understood algebra in high school and she didn't understand it now. What on earth did those letters stand for, anyway? And how could one side of an equation equal the other when they looked totally different?

Bored, she flipped on a Macy Gray CD and moved around her bedroom, plumping the white-on-white cushions on the wicker chair, stuffing a fallen rosebud into the cracked-glaze vase, rearranging the silver-framed photographs on the antique side table with the peeling cream paint.

Since their brief encounter at the barbershop, she hadn't heard from or seen Ben. What was he doing right now? Examining a baby? Setting a broken arm? Flirting with his new receptionist? Maybe not the latter. She'd glimpsed Barbara at the grocery store;

the nurse looked terrifyingly efficient but not very approachable.

Still, she found it pretty darn annoying that he'd known her nearly two weeks and in all that time he hadn't so much as suggested they go out for coffee. Dave, Gran's housecleaner, had invited her out three times for pizza. Kelly's boss, Ray, thought up a new way to impress her every time she ran into him, which mercifully wasn't frequently. Even the pharmacy student working at Blackwell's Drugstore for the summer had asked her to the movies. Almost every eligible man, and a few who weren't, had tried their luck. Geena had had a lot of practice declining invitations and she'd politely turned down every single one, waiting, hoping Ben would ask her out.

Well, she was tired of waiting and bored hanging around the house. If the mountain wouldn't come to Mohammed, she would go to the mountain.

The phone rang just as she was setting off for the clinic, and she hesitated, torn between going back and leaving it for the answering machine to pick up. When she was set on a course of action she hated to be delayed, even momentarily. She left it for the machine.

Maybe Ben hadn't asked her out because he thought she was only interested in partying. Well, she did like a good time, no question, and she could hardly spend all her Saturday nights playing cribbage with Gran. Most of her old friends still in town were married with young children, and their weekends were spent in domestic pursuits.

As she entered the clinic, Ben came out of his office to call in the next patient. For a second she wondered what was different about him, then a delighted and somewhat smug smile curved her lips as she realized he'd shaved off his mustache and goatee. Her delight turned to appreciation when she noticed the small but gorgeous cleft in his strongly defined chin.

She'd forgotten how tall he was. When she wore flat shoes, he topped her by a good four inches. His height was matched by a rugged physique, she noted as she took in his broad shoulders beneath his white cotton shirt. Brains and brawn. Whoever said the two were mutually exclusive had obviously not met Ben Matthews. Just seeing him made her pulse beat fast, sending a jungle message from her body to his.

He must have received the message, because he glanced up from his patient file. His face lit for a moment, then took on a suitably professional seriousness. "Geena, I was just trying to call you. If you can wait a few minutes I'd like to see you in my office."

"I can spare five minutes." Her heart singing, she

took a seat. Ben thought enough of her opinion to shave. Ben wanted to see her. Ben had tried to *call* her.

It was only after she'd read *People* magazine from cover to cover that he finally summoned her to his office. That was when she noticed his manner was formal, and she began to suspect this wasn't a social occasion, after all.

"Is something wrong?" she asked lightly. "If the receptionist isn't working out I could probably fit in a few hours a day." She would come back full-time in a flash if he needed her, she'd decided days ago.

"The receptionist is fine—excellent, in fact. The problem is you. I talked to the nutritionist in Simcoe."

Uh-oh. His hands were doing that steepling thing, and his expression was too bland to be friendly. She crossed her legs and swung the dangling foot in a small arc. "So?"

"So you know very well why I want to talk to you. You haven't made an appointment, let alone been evaluated. You haven't even had the blood samples taken. When I didn't get any results back, I called the lab. That's when I twigged to the probability that you hadn't seen the nutritionist, either. A phone call confirmed it."

"I'll get around to it."

He closed the file and rose. "Yes, you will, because you're going there now. With me."

"I most certainly am not." Men didn't order her around. Photographers cajoled, designers whined or gushed depending on their mood, and men who wanted to date her promised her the moon.

"I've got just forty minutes to personally escort you to the lab and the nutritionist," Ben said, coming around the desk to hold out his hand to her. "So when I say you're going with me, you'd better hop to it."

Okay, she hated to admit it, but being ordered by Ben sent a small thrill of excitement down her spine. That didn't mean she'd go meekly. "You can't just make me an appointment without my knowledge. I'm busy."

"Doing what?"

"None of your business." She remembered the high school books strewn around her bedroom, and her foot swung a little faster. She would die if he found out she was trying to finish high school at her age.

"Nothing is as important as your health," he said firmly. "I'm going to take you to Simcoe if I have to fling you over my shoulder and drag you to my car."

Although Geena could tell he wasn't serious, her

heart began to beat with a rapidity that had nothing to do with pills or stress. She arched one brow and gave him a cool smile. "As much as I might like that in other circumstances, this hardly seems the time or the place—Doctor."

Her smart-aleck comment brought a scowl to his face. He wrapped his fingers around hers in a hard, warm clasp and pulled her to her feet.

"Okay," she said, gathering her purse. "I'll come. Next time, though," she added, raising her chin, "I'd like a little notice."

The blood tests were a simple matter, but Geena hated walking into the nutritionist's office and seeing the older woman discreetly look her up and down. She didn't lecture, however; she just asked a million questions about Geena's general health and measured her height, weight and body fat. Then she made Geena write, as best she could remember, every item she'd eaten or drunk in the past seven days. This would be analyzed and used to determine whether her dietary intake provided her with adequate nutrition.

"Happy?" Geena asked as they drove to Hainesville in Ben's black Saab.

"Ecstatic. You're high maintenance, you know that?"

She inspected her nails, noting that the French

manicure needed redoing. "Nobody's ever complained before."

His lips pursed in a thin line. "You need a minder."

"Are you volunteering?" she asked, slanting him a smile.

"Ha! That'll be the day." Then he shook his head, as if he couldn't help but return her a smile. "Just see that you follow the nutritionist's advice."

"Or what?" she taunted, enjoying what had turned into a game.

"Or I'll turn you over my knee and paddle your behind."

"Promises, promises."

His mouth twitched, and Geena felt her body hum with a new energy. Ben might disapprove of her lifestyle, but he wasn't immune to her. *Oh, no,* she thought as she caught him sliding a sideways glance at her, *nowhere near immune.*

"Are you doing anything this Saturday?" she found herself asking. Simcoe for blood tests wasn't exactly a date, but he'd taken her out, and according to the rules of her personal etiquette, she could now return the favor.

"Not much. Did you have something in mind?"

"I'd like to go into Seattle and check out Nightmoves. It's the hottest club in town. I know the door bitch, so we wouldn't have to line up. We could walk right in.''

''Club,'' he repeated skeptically. ''As in, loud music, smoky atmosphere, sweaty bodies packed into a crowded room? Sorry, that's not my scene. How about having dinner with me, instead? I have a standing reservation at the Burger Shack on Friday night.'' He grinned. ''I know the girl behind the counter, and she'll give us extra thick milk shakes.''

Geena reluctantly shook her head. Today she'd had an orange for breakfast, one piece of crisp bread spread with a microthin layer of low-fat cream cheese for lunch, and she planned to have a lettuce salad, no dressing, for dinner. The last thing she wanted was Ben Matthews's misguided attempts to fatten her up. Or to torture herself with the sight and aroma of a big juicy burger. And onion rings. She hadn't had the Shack's deliciously spicy onion rings since just before she took off for New York at the tender age of sixteen. She salivated at the memory of that meal, remembered forever, destined never to be repeated.

''Thanks—but no, thanks,'' she said, more than a little regretful.

In Hainesville, Ben pulled up in front of Gran's house and walked Geena to the door. Instead of leaving, he stood there, hands in his pockets, bottom lip thrust out in contemplation. She hoped he was thinking of an alternative night out they could both enjoy.

"You said you liked helping out at the clinic," he said finally. His eyes searched hers as if testing her sincerity.

"Yes." She sincerely wanted to spend time around him.

"I have a proposition for you."

Proposition. "Sounds interesting. What is it?"

"Tod. He's out of the hospital after having chemotherapy. Carrie, his mom, is single and works two jobs to make ends meet. She has the baby to look after, as well, and doesn't have as much time as she'd like for Tod."

"What can I do?" Geena's buoyant spirits sank; she felt out of her depth just talking about this.

"Visit him. Read to him. He's feeling pretty down and could use a friend."

"He's a great kid, but surely he'd rather play with children his own age."

"His school friends visit, but not many nine-year-old boys are capable of sitting for long by a sickbed. That day at the clinic I saw the way Tod responded to you. I know he'd like to see you again."

Geena had grave doubts about whether she could really make a difference to a child with cancer, but for some reason Ben had faith in her. And Tod was a sweetie. How could she possibly say no?

"Okay."

"Thanks. I'll set it up with his mom." Ben smiled at her, his dark eyes glowing.

Geena was thrilled about gaining Ben's approval but she was also aware that a new feeling was spreading warmth through her. A feeling she hadn't experienced much in her hedonistic, self-indulgent life as a model.

She was going to help someone.

"HI, BEN." Eddie's voice sounded as close as next door.

"Hey, little buddy. How's it going?" Ben hunkered down in the beanbag in his rental house. The place was sparsely furnished, but he didn't mind. With his scarlet and blue Guatemalan rugs hanging on the white walls, woven baskets and simple furniture, he felt right at home.

"It's still raining, but I'm getting used to it," Eddie said. "I know many of the villagers by name, even picked up a word or two in the local dialect. But I haven't been able to get up the mountain to some of the more remote villages because the dirt roads are washed out."

"It would be worse if you were stuck up there.

Have you run into any medical problems you can't handle?''

"Not so far, although I'm worried about a patient in a village at the base of Volcán Santa Maria. A young woman—just a girl, really—in her first pregnancy. There are complications. I'd like to get her to the hospital in Quez for observation.''

Ben ran a hand through his hair, remembering only too well the frustration of inadequate medical facilities in the highlands. "You can only do what you can do," he said, knowing that Eddie, like Ben, would move mountains if necessary to get to a patient in need.

"A man is taking me up there tomorrow on burros," Eddie said, confirming Ben's thought.

"Good luck. By the way, how is Ysidro's broken leg healing? That was a nasty compound fracture.''

"I removed the cast a few days ago. You did a good job of straightening the limb.'' They talked for a few more minutes about Eddie's patients, then Eddie asked, "How's your supermodel?''

Ben chuckled. "Infuriating, exasperating... delightful. She's going to help me out with a young leukemia patient.''

"Ah, the plot thickens.'' Eddie's voice held teasing laughter. "Last time we talked you wanted nothing to do with her. What else is she helping you with, Doctor?''

"Nothing, so you can just forget it. We're very different people. She asked me to go with her to a nightclub. Can you imagine *me* at a nightclub? Naturally I declined.''

"Naturally," Eddie repeated dryly. "If a beautiful, rich, famous woman asked me out, I'd say no, too. Sometimes, big brother, you're too goal oriented. You're so focused on finding a suitable woman you could miss out on the love of your life. Are you seeing *anyone?*''

"Well, no. A few nice women have given me encouraging signs, but I haven't followed up.''

"And why not?''

"Um, not sure. I'll have to think about that.''

"I'll tell you why not," Eddie said. "It's because you're hung up on the supermodel.''

"Since when did you specialize in psychology?'' But Ben had to admit—at least to himself—Eddie might have a point. He did spend a lot of time thinking about Geena. He'd gone out of his way to take her to Simcoe for her blood work. And, as a doctor, he knew his physiological response to her couldn't be accounted for by anything other than sheer physical attraction.

"I guess I have to agree her company is stimulating."

Eddie laughed. "Get to know her. You may be surprised at what else she has to offer."

Frankly, he'd already been surprised by the interest she'd shown in Tod and Ben's other patients. "Maybe I'll do that. I suspect she's not quite as blasé about life as she makes out. Well, Eddie, I'd better go. This is costing you a fortune."

"You can't put a price on keeping in touch with your brother," Eddie said. "But I'll say goodbye. I have to see a man about a burro. Talk to you next week, Benny boy."

"Eddie, wait," Ben said quickly, suddenly and for no apparent reason reluctant to break the connection.

"Yes?"

"Er, nothing. Good luck with the pregnant girl." He paused. Despite their closeness, verbal expressions of affection were rare between him and his brother. Something prompted him to add, "Love ya, buddy."

A moment of silence. "Love you, too. Catch you later."

CHAPTER FIVE

"How LONG since you've been through your wardrobe and weeded things out, Kelly?" Geena demanded, her voice muffled by the clothes in her sister's closet.

"*I* never do, Gee. I leave that up to you since you get such pleasure from it." Kelly, flopped on her stomach on the bed, watched a beloved fuchsia blouse fly across the room and land on the carpet. "Hey, I want to keep that."

Erin, curled on the window seat, glanced up from a copy of *Vogue*. "Forget it, Kel. Once Geena gets started, there's no stopping her."

Geena pulled her head out of the closet and pushed rumpled auburn locks out of her eyes. "Frayed cuffs are bad for your image. Your clients will think either you don't know quality or you're no good at your job."

"But I love the color," Kelly protested, retrieving the offending blouse. "I admit, the cuffs are frayed, and it's way out-of-date, but I always feel so good wearing it.''

"That's what stores are for, Kel, so you can buy *new* clothes," Erin said. "Isn't that right, Geena?"

"Clothing stores are a grown-up woman's playground." Gently but firmly Geena took the blouse from Kelly and put it on the reject pile. "Why don't we all go to Seattle? Do some shopping, have dinner, hit Nightmoves in the evening. It'll be cool, just the three of us. I haven't been partying since before Milan and I'm dying for a little excitement."

"Sorry, you'll have to count me out." Erin glanced at her baby sleeping in a bassinet on the floor beside her. "I'm still breastfeeding Erik. I wouldn't want to leave him that long."

"What about you, Kel?" Geena raised her arms and did a little dance step. "Feel like a night on the town?"

Kelly's mouth twisted in a grimace. "Another jaunt without Max? I don't think so. He still secretly resents me for taking off to the Seychelles with you after Erin's wedding."

Geena's arms fell. She went to sit on the corner of the bed. "Things aren't so good with you two, are they? Have you tried counseling?"

Kelly gazed at the pillow her fingers were kneading and shook her head. "Max refuses. He won't bare his problems to strangers."

"I wish there were something we could do to help," Erin said, putting down the magazine.

Kelly sniffed, smiled and sat up. "Don't worry about Max and me; we'll be fine. I have a half day off next week, Gee. I'd love to go shopping then if you're free. You can help me find me a new blouse."

"It's a date. As for tonight, I guess I'll call Ronnie. He's always keen to go clubbing." Geena went to the closet and pulled out a row of skirts on hangers, which she held up for Kelly to see. "Which ones *haven't* you worn in the past year?"

Kelly winced. "All of them?"

"*Ronnie,* huh?" Erin exchanged a grin with Kelly. "Geena, are you trying to make a certain doctor jealous?"

"For your information, Ronnie is gay," Geena said, stripping skirts off hangers and throwing them on the reject pile. She glanced at her sisters. "Do you think if I went out with another man Ben would be jealous?"

"He's red-blooded, hetero and single," Erin said. "How could he not be?"

Kelly rolled off the bed and quietly began putting her skirts on their hangers. "Why don't you ask Ben to go out with you tonight?"

"I did. He's allergic to techno music. He did invite me to the Burger Shack with him, though."

Erin and Kelly stared at her. "And the reason you didn't go?" Erin demanded.

Geena rolled her eyes. "Burgers, fries...*fat*. Do I need to say more?"

"Geena," Kelly and Erin said in unison. Kelly added, "You, of all people, can afford to swallow a few fat grams."

Erin chimed in. "For God's sake, girl, true love demands sacrifices."

Hands raised in self-defense, Geena stemmed their attack. "It's just a minor setback. We haven't found common ground yet."

"What would that be?" Kelly wondered. "He's a doctor, dedicated to healing, and you're a model, dedicated to fashion."

Geena felt the truth of Kelly's words in her bones, and just as deeply, she rejected them. "People aren't just their professions," she declared. "There's more to each of us." In her case, she just had to discover what that was.

"Speaking of fashion..." She paused. "You know I'm helping Greta Vogler organize a fashion show. We need more models."

"Oh, no." Erin laughed. "I just had a baby."

"I've had four," Kelly said.

"You both look fantastic. Come on, don't make me beg."

"Oh, all right. If Kelly will."

"I'm too short."

"This is Hainesville, not New York."

"Okay, okay."

"Do you want teenagers?" Erin asked. "I'll bet Miranda would love to be involved."

"Great idea," Geena said, and turned to Kelly. "Hey, where are you going with those skirts?"

Kelly was attempting to sneak the skirts into the other end of the closet. "You're too ruthless, Gee. The blouse was worn, but I can't throw out a perfectly good article of clothing just because I never wear it. Wait till you have a family and have to live on a budget."

A sudden cry from the bassinet had the three sisters' immediate attention.

"Hello, sweetie pie," Geena crooned, picking Erik up and giving him a cuddle before handing him to Erin.

"Right on schedule," Erin said, glancing at her watch. She reached under her sweater to unhook her nursing bra. "Every three hours, he's hungry. I swear you could set a clock by him."

"Speaking of time, I'd better run if I'm going into Seattle," Geena said. She hugged Kelly and trailed an affectionate hand down Erin's long blond hair. "See you later."

"Take care."

"Have fun tonight."

"Thanks, I will. Kelly, that pile goes directly to Goodwill. Erin, watch her."

"Kelly…"

Geena heard Erin's warning even as she moved toward the door, and she exited, laughing.

GEENA WASN'T laughing when she dragged herself home in the wee hours of Sunday morning. Her lungs hurt from inhaling passive smoke, her ears rang from hours of deafening music, and she had a headache. Her last thought before falling into bed was to wonder if she was sick. This was the first time she'd failed to enjoy herself doing the town.

Gran was at the stove stirring something in the frying pan when Geena lounged into the kitchen the next morning in a satin dressing gown. Gran assessed her through her oversize blue plastic glasses. "Had a late night, I take it. Drink too much?"

Geena got herself a glass of water and downed a couple of painkillers. "I didn't drink or smoke or *anything* last night. I didn't feel like indulging at all. In fact, the whole idea repulsed me."

"After I had my heart attack last year I knew I'd

had a lucky escape and vowed to take better care of myself," Gran said. "Maybe your body is telling you not to abuse it anymore." She carried a plate of scrambled eggs and sausages to the table, where a stack of buttered toast and a bowl of fresh fruit salad were already set out. "Come and eat."

"Oh, Gran, you shouldn't have gone to so much trouble," Geena protested. "You know I don't have breakfast."

"From now on you do," Gran said firmly. "Dr. Matthews dropped by yesterday to give me a copy of the diet the nutritionist recommended for you. Apparently, the analysis showed you weren't getting adequate protein or fat, and you're lacking certain minerals. He asked me to make sure you followed the nutritionist's advice. He seemed to think you might forget if left to your own devices."

"I'm not a child," Geena muttered.

"Then start acting like a grown-up and eat."

Geena tried, just to please her grandmother. She had a few forkfuls of egg, a quarter of a piece of toast and a small bowl of fruit salad. Finally, she couldn't eat another bite, and pushed her plate away. "Sorry, Gran, that's it for me."

Gran shook her head and made a tsking sound. "What am I going to do with you, girl?"

Geena smiled. "Well, I guess you won't be putting

me to bed without my dinner the way you used to when I was little.''

A pair of lines appeared between Gran's gray eyebrows. ''Did I do that?''

''Only when I got too wild and wouldn't stop carrying on even after Gramps was called in.''

''You used to get so wound up, trying to keep up with your older sisters. You were always doing something crazy to get attention.'' She frowned harder, worried. ''Oh, Geena, if I'm responsible for you getting too thin—''

''Stop, Gran,'' Geena said, sorry she'd brought the subject up. She rose and went to hug her grandmother. ''It's not your fault I've got an eating problem—'' She broke off, paced across the room. ''Not that I *have* an eating problem. Because I don't. I just watch my weight. Nothing wrong with that. I have to in my line of work.''

''Never mind, Geena, love,'' Gran soothed. ''Everything's going to be fine. Now, I'm going to church. Would you like to come?''

''Yes, maybe I would.'' She'd never been especially religious, but she did wonder if she'd ever relive the joy she'd experienced in the presence of the light. Many people found spiritual guidance in church; maybe she would, too.

An hour later, Geena was seated on the polished

wooden pew, which was both hard and cool to the touch. The stained-glass window over the altar cast jewel-colored shadows on the choir and the snowy linen of the pastor's surplice. She sang hymns familiar from childhood, paid attention to the sermon and bowed her head with the rest of the congregation. But while she found some comfort in the nostalgia of days past, she knew with a hollow feeling that she wasn't going to find her spiritual path in a bricks-and-mortar symbol of the truth she'd experienced firsthand.

When the chords of the last hymn faded and people rose to leave, Geena whispered to Gran, ''I've got to go.'' She slipped out of the pew and all but ran down the center aisle and out the double doors, into the sun.

On the steps she paused and gulped in air. Oh, the blessed sun, the trees, the flowers and grass. Moisture rose in her eyes, and she thanked God for the natural world. She heard the voices behind her, and without looking to see who was there, she walked swiftly down the steps and along the sidewalk, not stopping until she'd reached the little footbridge in the park that took her across the river and onto the path beside the flowing water.

There she slowed at last, and removed her shoes and stockings to feel the cool moist earth beneath her bare feet. Her heart slowed, too, and once the pounding in her ears stopped she could hear the gentle chirping of birds among the dappled green and the rustle of some small animal in the undergrowth.

In a sunny clearing by the river she plunked herself on a mossy log and sat very still, wanting just to *be*. Her eyes shut, and gradually she fell into a meditative trance, relishing the sun on her face, breathing in the scent of water and rock, vegetation and earth. She had no idea how much time passed. Minutes and seconds had no meaning. In the forest, she felt closer to the light than anywhere else. Peace enveloped her, buoyed her spirit, calmed her soul.

A noise, an air current, *something* roused her from the depths of her subconscious and brought her to the surface. Inhaling deeply, she opened her eyes. Ben was jogging along the path. At the edge of the clearing he saw her and stopped abruptly.

FOR BEN, the morning had started like any other Sunday. He had rolled out of bed and donned shorts and a T-shirt to go for a run. The day couldn't have been more perfect; the sky was the clear deep blue of late summer, and the air soft and warm. He'd jogged along the river to the park before looping back.

At the house, he'd stretched, showered and

changed, then flipped on the radio in the kitchen while he made breakfast. The aroma of freshly ground coffee tickled his nostrils, reminding him of the coffee plantations near his Guatemalan village. And then, like a pinprick to the brain, he heard the radio newscaster say the word "Guatemala."

He put down the kettle and turned up the radio, thinking the report must be of the recent election in that country. Instead, he listened in growing horror as news unfolded of an earthquake in the western highlands:

"Six point three on the Richter scale. The epicenter was located outside Quezaltenango in a small Mayan village already besieged by heavy rainfall and flooding. Hundreds are dead and thousands missing, as aftershocks of the worst quake in fifty years continue to rock the area."

The spoon in Ben's hand clattered to the floor. *Eddie.*

The phone rang. Ben jumped.

His hand shaking, he picked up the receiver. "Hello?" His voice sounded strange, hoarse, not like him at all.

"Ben, there's been an earthquake—" His mother's voice, thick with fear, wobbly with tears, broke off.

Ben dragged a hand across his face at the thought

of what she must be going through. "I just caught the news on the radio. Have you heard from Eddie?"

"I was hoping he'd called you." She started to sob.

"Mom, try not to worry. We don't have details yet."

"The village was at the epicenter. How can I not worry?"

"Eddie's like a cat with nine lives," Ben said. "He always manages to land on his feet. Remember when we thought he was lost while caving? He came through then, didn't he?" He tried to speak with assurance, but the cold ball of fear in his stomach put a tremor in his voice.

"This is different."

He had to admit it was. "Is Dad with you?"

"He went into town earlier. Unless he had the car radio on, he doesn't know yet." Another sob racked her voice. "Oh, Ben!"

"I'll call International Médicos and see what I can find out. Maybe he's safe and sound on a weekend jaunt to Guatemala City." He attempted a chuckle, but it sounded like a rusty gate. "I'll call you back as soon as I hear anything. I love you, Mom."

He hung up and dialed the number of International Médicos in Guatemala City, even though he was certain the office would be shut on Sunday. While the phone rang, he glanced at the calendar. September 5, the day the world shifted. Finally he gave up and called international directory assistance for the number of the police station in Quezaltenango. Telephone lines were down, and he couldn't get through. He tried the hospital and several more authorities in Guatemala City, but no one knew anything of Dr. Edward Matthews. All was chaos and confusion.

Dazed, he flipped on CNN. The pictures of damaged houses and bodies lying in the rubble made his stomach churn. The camera flashed to the raging river, showing dead animals and pieces of buildings being swept downstream. His throat closed up as he contemplated the fate of his villagers. How many of the people he'd come to know and love were dead?

He realized it was illogical, but he felt guilty for having escaped the destruction. What right did he have to be alive when so many were dead and injured?

And Eddie... The sense of guilt deepened. Eddie wouldn't even *be* in Guatemala if it hadn't been for Ben. He'd encouraged Eddie to apply to the organization; he'd recommended his brother. Ben dragged a hand over his face. Oh, God, what had he done?

He couldn't sit still, couldn't stay in the house another minute. He left, running along the river path. He didn't notice the blue sky or the soft warm air.

He was running, running, chased by jumbled images of the earthquake and revolving fears for his brother's safety. That Eddie should be alive seemed impossible, yet Ben's mind couldn't accept the alternative. He was frozen in a limbo of uncertainty, unable to grieve or to hope.

Then he came around a bend in the path to find Geena sitting on a mossy log in the clearing. With her slight figure in a pale-green dress and light sparking off her auburn hair, she seemed an unlikely combination of ethereal and earthy, a wood nymph in a timeless setting.

Ben, his mind in turmoil from the news of the disaster in Guatemala, wished he could jog past unnoticed. The frantic call from his mother and his attempts to reassure her of Eddie's safety had left his stomach knotted in fear and sapped his ability to relate to others. He had a split second in which to make up his mind to nod and run past, but then she glanced up, and the sight of her made him stumble to a halt.

He saw her little start, no more than a blink, as she became aware of him. The deep blue of her irises was like the sky itself. Something flowed between them. She smiled at him, and the gesture loosened his limbs. He walked toward her.

CHAPTER SIX

HE SAT on the log beside her and attempted to make conversation. "I didn't figure you for a nature lover."

"It's come as something of a surprise to me, too." Head tilted, frowning, she studied him. "Are you all right?"

"Yeah, fine." Then he realized he was leaning forward, elbows on his knees, twisting his hands together. He made himself relax, tried to rub away the tension that was driving lines between his brows.

She gazed at him, waiting.

He breathed out through his mouth. "Okay, I'm not fine. Did you hear the news this morning? There was an earthquake in Guatemala. The village I used to live and work in was at the epicenter."

"Oh, I'm so sorry. I guess some of the people you knew would have been injured, even killed. Wait a minute!" French polished nails pressed against cinnamon-colored lips. "Your brother!"

"Yes...Eddie." His voice broke, and he needed a

minute before he could speak again. "I haven't been able to get in touch with him." He spread his hands, unable to go on.

She touched his arm. Her slender fingers were pale against his tanned skin and made him aware of her as a woman. He wanted, yet didn't want, to be distracted from Eddie.

"He's probably all right," he said. "Communication with those small villages isn't good at the best of times. I'm sure I'll hear in a day or two that he's fine. He'll be so busy helping others that he hasn't checked in himself."

"I'm sure you're right."

"I just talked to him two days ago," Ben said, staring into the river. "When I went to hang up I had the strangest reluctance to say goodbye."

"You had a premonition."

"Oh, I don't know about that." He scraped moss off the log and crumbled it between his fingers. He felt a strong urge to talk about his brother, and Geena's oddly calming presence encouraged him to open up. "I've never told anyone this before, but Eddie is the reason I became a doctor."

"Really? Why is that?"

"When I was twelve years old and Eddie was six, there was a meningitis outbreak. Eddie got sick, really sick. We thought…he wasn't going to make it."

Ben's clenched hand buried itself in the palm of his other hand. "Another boy in our town died. I felt helpless and terrified. I realized how easily the disease could also kill my little brother."

"What happened?" Geena asked. "He survived, obviously."

"Our family doctor recognized his symptoms and put him straight into the hospital. The doctors gave him massive doses of antibiotics and brought him from the brink of death. To me, it seemed nothing less than a miracle. I decided then I was going to become a doctor and perform miracles myself." He paused. "I also vowed to look after my brother so that nothing could hurt him again." Ben kicked the fallen moss away with his running shoe. "I haven't performed too well on that score."

"Ben!" Geena took his hands in hers. "It's not your fault Eddie was caught in an earthquake. You can't blame yourself."

"I realize that," he said heavily, not wanting to meet her gaze. "I just wish I could believe it."

"You know, Ben..." Geena hesitated. "Death is not the end."

He gazed at her, not comprehending. "What do you mean?"

"I mean, there's a life after death. I've seen it."

"Geena," he said, appalled she would bring up

her near-death experience now. "I've explained that to you."

She sighed. "Never mind that then." She rose suddenly and dragged him to his feet. "Come with me."

"Where are you taking me?"

"You'll see." She pulled him along the path to a tiny cove where the current had eroded the muddy bank to create a backwater. Swimming in and about the exposed tree roots was a mallard family—mother, father and four ducklings. Since it was late summer, the youngsters were nearly full grown and almost as big as their parents. When they saw Geena and Ben, the ducks swam, quacking, to the bank, the babies just as adept in fending for themselves as the older ducks.

"See the young ones?" she said. "They stick close to their parents, but if you saw them on their own, you'd think they were grown-up, wouldn't you?"

Ben nodded at the simple analogy. "Eddie's twenty-nine. I guess you could call him an adult."

"*I'm* twenty-nine," Geena said, smiling. "I'm an adult. Therefore he certainly is, too. And responsible for himself."

"Maybe." Ben smiled, delighted to turn her lesson back on her without detracting from the value of it. "But we've already established that *you* need taking care of."

She swatted him lightly with a twig. "In *your* opinion. And we've already established that you tend to mother your little brother."

Unbelievably, Ben was able to laugh. She had him there.

They walked along the river trail. "How was your night on the town?" Ben asked.

"Oh, that," she said as if speaking of a long-ago event. "It was great." Then she shook her head. "What am I saying? It was awful. The music gave me a headache and the smoke hurt my lungs. I felt...disconnected." She glanced at the peaceful greenery and the river flowing. "This is better."

"I'd agree with you there."

She sighed. "I hardly know myself anymore."

"Is that bad?"

"Yes. No. I don't know."

She sounded so lost that without thinking he put his arm around her shoulder. Her luminous blue gaze lit with recognition of shared feelings. This was not flirtation but something new, an openness to growing affection. Under other circumstances he would have kissed her. God knows, he'd fantasized about that, and more, many a long night. But the sharp pain of

Eddie's disappearance colored his emotions, and he didn't want their first kiss tainted with grief.

Eventually they reached Ben's house.

Geena stopped and turned to him. "Do you want me to stay with you for a while?"

Part of him wanted that very much. "Actually, I need to make some phone calls." He hesitated. "Of all people, I'm glad it was you I ran into today."

She nodded, seeming to understand, then took his hand and squeezed. Ben felt a strong urge to put both arms around her. To hold her and be held. And he might have, if he hadn't been afraid he would break down.

Instead, he drew back. "I'll call you. About Tod, I mean. Carrie suggested Wednesday or Thursday next week."

"Either day would be fine." She smiled faintly, already backing away. "Ciao."

GEENA GAZED at the animated faces of the women seated around the meeting table of the ladies' auxiliary. They'd happily exchanged their bingo night for a fashion show, contrary to Greta's dire predictions, and divided themselves into subcommittees to investigate music, flowers and refreshments. Candy's Boutique and Briony's Women's Wear were charged with coming up with a range of fall fashions, and

Geena agreed to take care of the models and act as general consultant.

"All right, ladies," Geena said. "Who fancies herself on the catwalk? We've got enough younger women and teens, but we also need mature women." Stunned silence. "Come on. We've titled the show Real Fashions for Real Women. You don't have to be a professional model or have a perfect figure to participate."

Mabel Gribble banged her gavel, as she did at every possible opportunity. "If none of you ninnies will volunteer, I will. Put my name down, Geena. I was known for having a great set of legs in my day." She glared around the table as if to silence any dissenters.

"Excellent," Geena said, and wrote Mabel's name in lavender ink.

With a nervous giggle, Doreen tentatively raised her hand. "I wouldn't mind, if you think I'd be good enough. I plan to lose ten pounds in the next two weeks."

"You'll be fabulous, Doreen. Don't worry about your weight. We'll find you beautiful clothes to fit. Who else?" She gazed around expectantly, but no one else was game enough to speak up. "Greta, how about you?"

Her ex-teacher looked startled. "Me? Definitely not. I'm the last person to model clothing."

Geena gave up and moved on. With a little prodding, several other women agreed to model, and the renewed excitement forced Mabel to bang her gavel repeatedly.

"Ladies! We need to settle on a date." Mabel's bosom rested comfortably on her plump arms as she glanced around the table. "How does the tenth of October sound? That gives us a good month to prepare."

"The high school reunion is scheduled for that date," Greta informed her.

Mabel consulted a pocket calendar. "In that case we could try for a week earlier, on the third."

"We'd never be ready on time," Rachel Bigelow, from the florist shop, said.

"She's right," Geena concurred, and Briony nodded in agreement. "How about the week after…what's that, the seventeenth?"

"Any objections?" Mabel swept her gaze around the table, looking for objectors, and found none. She banged her gavel again. "The seventeenth it is. Thank you, ladies, and good afternoon."

Geena raised a hand. "Excuse me."

"Yes?" Mabel held her gavel poised above the table.

Geena rose to her feet so everyone could see her. "I guess you've all heard by now about the earthquake in Guatemala. Many people are homeless, others in need of food and medicine. I was wondering if your next fund-raising event could donate some money to a Guatemala relief fund."

"That's a wonderful idea. Very thoughtful," Mabel said. "But we won't be planning another charity event until spring. That might be too late to be of assistance."

"Oh, I see." Geena sat down. In that case, she would make her check to the relief agency a little bigger.

"Ooh, I know." Doreen's hand shot up. "Why don't we use the money from the fashion show for the Guatemalans? Then we could plan our spring fund-raiser around the maternity wing." She flinched under the force of Greta's outraged glare. "Sorry, Greta."

"The situation in Guatemala is tragic, I agree," Greta said. "But we need to take care of our own. We don't even know those Guatemalans."

"Dr. Matthews does," Geena replied. "His brother is missing over there."

"Oh, then we must help," Martha Haines said, to murmurs of general approbation. "After all, Simcoe has a perfectly good maternity ward already."

Greta fixed Geena with an icy stare. "Just because you've set your cap at the man doesn't mean the whole town has to turn itself inside out for him."

"Set my cap!" Geena sputtered. "Where on earth did you get such a ridiculous idea?"

The ladies' auxiliary erupted into vigorous debate, some members concerned with the fund-raising event, most arguing about whether or not Geena was after the doctor, and if so, whether he would be right for her.

Mabel's gavel beat a staccato on the table. "Can we please save discussion of Geena's love life until after the meeting? Dr. Matthews's brother was at the epicenter of the quake. As a show of support for our town doctor, I move we follow Geena's suggestion and give the proceeds of the fashion show to the medical outfit Ben and his brother volunteered with—what's it called?"

"International Médicos," Geena said. "But I should point out that this wasn't actually my suggestion. Even though I agree."

Martha Haines stuck up her hand. "I'll second that."

"All in favor?" Mabel demanded. She counted the show of hands that went up around the table. "Against?" More hands went up.

"Six for, six against," Mabel said. "As chairperson I cast the deciding vote.'' Her frown softened, and she smoothed her well-coiffed silver curls. ''Dr. Matthews prescribed me a wonderful new medication that fixed my ulcer right up. I vote aye!''

''I'm sorry,'' Geena said to Greta as they exited the town hall after the meeting. ''I didn't mean for that to happen.''

Greta's mouth twisted as though she were sucking on a lemon. ''You Hanson girls! Always wrecking my plans for a maternity wing. You have it in for me, don't you?''

''No, honestly,'' Geena said, dismayed. Last year Erin had inadvertently stopped Greta's attempts to get the town council to pay for a maternity wing, but to her knowledge, Kelly had never done anything to thwart Greta's dream.

Greta climbed into her green Ford station wagon and slammed the door.

''Is it still okay if I drop by later to pick up that GED preparation manual you promised me?'' Geena called through the open window.

Greta's answering scowl Geena took as a yes. She backed away from the car with a sigh. No matter what, she seemed to rub that woman the wrong way. And vice versa.

Geena cast a resigned gaze to the heavens. *I'm trying, Mom. But she's more trying.*

CARRIE WAKEFIELD answered the door with the harried look of a single mom who had a seriously ill child and not enough time or money. Her long black hair was disheveled from being pulled at by the sniveling baby in her arms.

"Hi, Geena. Come on in." She backed away from the door, giving Geena a glimpse of a tiny living room strewn with toys and a sofa buried beneath a jumble of clean laundry. Colored crystals were strung the length of the window, making rainbows on the walls.

"Thanks. Hi, there," Geena cooed to the baby and tickled him under his chin. He smiled shyly and turned his face into his mother's neck. "I like your blouse," she said to Carrie.

"Thanks. This little munchkin is Billy. He's got a cold." Carrie sighed. "He's *always* got a cold. Tod's in his room," she added, adjusting the sniffling child on her hip. "Second door on the right down the hall. He's still kinda sick from the chemo. He's hardly eaten a bite all week. I was really glad when Dr. Matthews told him you would visit. Tod's been so down."

"I'll see if I can cheer him up."

Despite her confident words, Geena felt more than a little trepidation as she trod the worn green carpet to Tod's room. She wasn't trained in dealing with cancer patients. What on earth could *she* say or do that would make Tod feel better? She knocked on his door, and a small voice told her to come in.

Tod lay in bed, his pale, drawn face dimly illuminated by a table lamp. The curtains were shut, and even the aromatherapy oil burner atop the battered dresser couldn't disguise the stale odor of a sickroom.

Geena hid her shock and put on a cheerful smile. "Hey, Tod. How are you feeling?"

"Who are you?" he asked, listless.

"Don't you remember me from the clinic? I'm Geena, a friend of Dr. Matthews. He sent over a book for you. Shall I open the curtains so you can take a look?"

Tod shrugged, uninterested in the book, but his expression perked up at the mention of Ben. "Dr. Ben showed me a liver in a jar when we were at the hospital. He said it was pickled even before the hospital got it."

Geena suppressed a smile. "He's nice, isn't he?"

"Is he going to visit me?"

"Um, he's awfully busy being a doctor. But I'm sure he's looking forward to your next visit at the clinic."

At the mixture of disappointment and hope on Tod's face, Geena diagnosed a serious case of hero worship. She pushed back the curtains and opened the window to let in fresh air. From the neighboring yard came the sounds of children playing, and she winced, knowing Tod must hear it, too, and feel keenly the contrast between healthy children and himself, ill and confined to bed.

She sat on a straight-backed chair beside the bed and cast around for something to talk about. "Heard any good jokes lately?"

He thought for a moment. "What did the sand say to the rain?"

"I give up."

"Stop, or my name will be mud." He grinned, stretching his freckles across his nose.

"That's a good one. Where did Napoleon keep his armies?"

"I dunno."

"Up his sleevies. Is that a pyramid?" she asked, spying a small wooden object on the upturned milk crate that functioned as a bedside table.

Tod nodded. "Mom says it has healing powers in case the white light doesn't work. At least it's not as stinky as that oil she burns for arom…aroma—"

"Aromatherapy." Geena leaned forward, forearms on her knees. "I love essential oils. I'm not sure if they heal, but they can't do you any harm."

"*You* smell pretty good," Tod said grudgingly.

"Ah, well, when it comes to smelling good, French perfume beats oils any day." Silence fell. Tod gazed at her, not even blinking. "Okay." She brought the book out of her tote bag. "Shall we find out what this book has to say?"

Geena shifted her chair so Tod could see the pictures and then she started to read. Pretty soon she was feeling uncomfortable about the story. She was no expert, but a detailed description of the effects of chemo, which Tod must know only too well, didn't seem the best way to cheer up a sick child. Tod's face got longer and longer. Still she plodded on, thinking Ben must know what he was doing.

"Do you want to see my pet grasshopper?"

With relief, she closed the book. "Sure. What's his name?"

"Arnie." Tod pulled himself up in bed and reached for a cigar box on the side table. "I'm training him." As the little boy cautiously slid back the lid of the cigar box, his wan face took on greater animation. "Okay, Arnie, be good," he warned, cupping the grasshopper in his hand. "Show Geena how you can walk along the pencil."

Geena watched, fascinated, as Tod, his tongue firmly clamped between his lips, carefully placed Arnie at the end of an unsharpened pencil. The grasshopper shifted his front feet minutely while his antennae lashed the air.

"Atta boy," Tod said in a low, encouraging tone, his eyes at bug level. "Okay...now slowly come toward me...."

The grasshopper leaped into the air, but instead of moving toward Tod, he jumped straight at Geena. She shrieked, batting at the whirring insect, and laughed when he landed on her shoulder. In a swift movement she dropped her cupped hand over the grasshopper and handed him back to Tod.

"Want to see that again?" the boy asked, eager to repeat the experiment.

Geena put a hand over her heart. "I think Arnie's had enough excitement for one day. Do you have any other pets?"

"Nah." His delighted grin faded to a wistful sadness. "I wanted a dog, but Mom says we can't afford one. And even if we could, she doesn't have time to look after it, and I'm not well enough."

Poor little guy. "You've got a great grasshopper. I'd like to see that trick again after all. Can you show me?"

Tod's face lit, and he happily showed off Arnie's dubious accomplishments until Geena noticed the sun had gone from the window. "I guess I should get going. It's probably time for your dinner."

"I'm not hungry."

Geena remembered what his mom had said. "You need to eat so your body has the strength to fight off disease."

"Mom makes yucky stuff like Brussels sprouts."

"Brussels sprouts are good for you, just what a growing boy needs. Dr. Matthews says—"

"What? What does Dr. Ben say?"

"He says you need to eat properly to be healthy."

"Oh." Tod sighed and slumped on the pillows.

Geena debated with herself. When she spoke next she wasn't sure if she'd won or lost. "Do you like hamburgers?"

"Yeah."

"I happen to know that Dr. Matthews eats dinner at the Burger Shack on Fridays. Do you feel well enough to go there with me? My treat."

"You bet!"

"As long as it's okay with your mom," Geena cautioned.

"She won't mind," Tod assured her. "Not if it means I'm going to eat."

CHAPTER SEVEN

BEN PUT A QUARTER in the mini jukebox, selected Garth Brooks, then leaned back in his booth at the Burger Shack while he waited for his order to be filled. Four teenage girls in the corner were sipping shakes and giving him the eye, giggling when they saw him look their way. He smiled in their direction, then, looking past the girls through the window, felt his heart bump. Geena was coming up the walk, Tod in tow.

Busy at the clinic and preoccupied with tracking down news of his brother, Ben hadn't seen Geena since Sunday, but he'd been thinking about her all week. About the incredible blue of her eyes, the incandescence of her smile, her intriguing combination of fragility and strength. He'd planned to drop by her house after he ate. Unbelievably, she'd come *here*, to the Burger Shack.

When Geena pushed the door open her head was down, and she was laughing at something Tod said. Then she glanced around, and her gaze found Ben's.

She smiled, and Ben's heart did a slow flip. He lifted a hand in greeting. Geena and Tod wove through the crowded restaurant to his booth.

"Hi," she said. "Mind if we join you?"

"My pleasure," he replied. "Hi, Tod. How're you doing, buddy?"

"Hi, Dr. Ben. I'm okay." The boy slid into the opposite seat ahead of Geena. Ben studied his pale face, transformed by excitement, and gave Geena full marks for taking the boy out for a change of pace.

Geena handed Tod a menu. "Order whatever you like."

Ben's hamburger and onion rings came, along with a large chocolate shake—food he wasn't going to tire of easily after two years of eating mainly rice and beans.

"My stomach doesn't feel too good," Tod said. "Maybe I won't have anything, after all."

"I'll just have a diet cola," Geena said to the waitress, who'd pulled out her pad and pencil.

"You need to eat to help your body recover," Ben said to Tod, wishing he could say the same to Geena.

"She's not eating," Tod said.

Ben unwrapped his burger, releasing aromatic steam, and saw Geena's nostrils flare. She *wanted* to eat, but was holding herself back out of some fool notion that she was overweight. He'd consulted with the nutritionist after Geena's appointment, and she'd told him she didn't think Geena was a true anorexic; she was starving herself for professional reasons. The solution seemed obvious to Ben—get out of the profession. Geena probably wouldn't see it that way.

"As your doctor, I'm ordering you to eat."

She laughed, completely undeterred. "You can order all you want, but I don't have to obey."

"Neither do I," Tod said in solidarity with his new friend, apparently having decided that if Geena could rebel, so could he.

Ben threw Geena a now-see-what-you've-done look and in a less stern tone said to Tod, "You're right, I can't force you to eat. But it's my professional opinion that you and Geena could use some extra nourishment. Plus, I hate to eat alone, so I'd take it as a personal favor if you would join me."

Spoken to with the respect normally accorded to adults, Tod softened. "Okay. Geena, if I eat, will you join me?" he asked politely in an inadvertent parody of Ben.

Way to go, Tod. Ben raised his eyebrows at Geena, daring her to refuse.

She laughed and threw her hands up in gracious surrender. "I'll eat. You're a very persuasive fellow," she said to Tod, though Ben had the gratifying feeling her remarks were directed at him.

Ben turned to the waitress, still patiently standing there, pencil poised over her pad. "Two hamburgers and two milk shakes, please."

"Diet cola," Geena interjected.

"Can I have a strawberry shake?" Tod asked.

As the waitress turned to go, Geena added, "And a large order of onion rings." Ben smiled and she shrugged. "Might as well be hung for a sheep as a lamb."

"Are we having lamb?" Tod said, suddenly alarmed.

"No, sweetie," Geena reassured him. "That's just an expression."

"Did you read the book I sent over?" Ben asked.

Geena and Tod exchanged a look. "We started on it," Geena said diplomatically. "Have you read it?"

"I skimmed it." Ben tried to decipher the silent message in her eyes. Somehow the book had failed to live up to his good intentions. He'd talk to her about it later.

"Have you heard from your brother?" she asked.

She spoke lightly, and he was grateful, because that enabled him to say, "Not yet," as though Eddie had simply gone out of town unexpectedly.

"I showed Geena my pet grasshopper," Tod said, oblivious to undercurrents.

"He can do tricks," Geena added, and the conversation revolved around the talented Arnie until Geena's and Tod's food arrived.

Now that he had his burger in front of him, Tod tucked in with an appetite. Geena stared at hers as though it might bite her, instead of the other way around.

"How long since you had one of these?" Ben asked. He'd finished his own and had his eye on her onion rings.

"I believe it was sometime last century."

"Eat up." He took an onion ring. "Quick, before it all disappears."

Geena looked from Ben to Tod, who said encouragingly, his voice muffled by hamburger, "It's good."

She swallowed, and Ben knew she had to be salivating. The wrapper fell away, and she picked up the hamburger, the bun shiny with grease and oozing special sauce, and slowly she raised it to her mouth. She took a bite, and her eyes closed in rapturous delight. "Oh! Oh, my."

The couple at the next table turned to stare.

"Eating's such a pleasurable experience for you I wonder you don't do it more often," Ben murmured.

"It's a matter of discipline. How're you doing, Tod?" Geena asked. "Is your stomach feeling any better?"

"Lots better," he replied happily. "This sure beats Brussels sprouts. Thanks for bringing me here."

She stroked the blond curl that sprang from his cowlick. "I'm glad you could come."

"Want to choose a song?" Ben asked Tod, digging in his pocket for a couple of quarters.

Tod had fun pressing buttons, but Ben was pretty sure the boy hadn't grasped the relationship between his selection and what came over the speakers, because the music he chose was a romantic ballad.

"Yuck." Tod glared at the jukebox.

"It's beautiful." Geena smiled dreamily at Ben through half-shut eyes as she swayed to the song.

Get to know her, Eddie had told him. Well, why not? Ben had a feeling there was a lot to learn about Geena Hanson. For a glamour babe she seemed to genuinely care about a sick boy. That made her okay in his book.

Tod yawned and pushed away the scraps of his dinner. "I'm tired."

"Time to go," Ben said, and turned to Geena. "Are you ready?"

In spite of Geena's obvious enjoyment of her food, she only ate half of her hamburger and a few of the onion rings. Ben was pleased she'd eaten that much.

Geena nodded. "I left my car at Gran's, and we

walked the few blocks here. I thought Tod could use the fresh air, but I didn't think about afterward."

"Come on. I'll take you both back."

Ben drove Tod home to a grateful mom, then cruised through the quiet streets toward Geena's house. He found himself driving slowly, not wanting to say good-night.

"It's still early," he said, one hand draped over the wheel. "Do you want to catch a movie?"

"I can't," she said, crossing her arms over her stomach. "I...I promised I'd play cards with Gran."

He raised one eyebrow sardonically. "As an excuse, that ranks right up there with washing your hair. Besides, I happen to know that your grandmother plays bridge with Edna and Martha on Friday nights." He paused and looked more closely at her. "Are you feeling okay?"

"Fine. Anyway, I don't have to explain myself," she said, putting her chin in the air. "Men line up to take me out. They book a date weeks in advance."

Ben pulled up in front of her grandmother's big Victorian house and took a pocket calendar out of his wallet. "What are you doing Saturday, October tenth? That's three weeks away," he teased. "Is that enough time to satisfy your ego?"

"The tenth? I'm busy that night."

"You're kidding me." He got out and noticed she

was waiting for him to come around and open her door. Why not? he thought with a shrug. He liked acting the gentleman, and so few women allowed it these days.

He was a little surprised, though, when she brushed straight past him and glided up the walk, her perfume trailing behind her like a siren's song.

He followed, his long stride matching hers. Overtaking her, he leaned on the doorjamb, blocking her from putting her key in the lock. "How about the Saturday following the tenth?"

"The seventeenth?" She inserted her key in the lock. "I've got something on that night, too."

"Playing hard to get, are we?" He reached for her. "Why don't you tell me when..." Then words failed him as her scent filled his nostrils and her slender curves took shape beneath his hands. He bent forward and just brushed her lips with his. The brief kiss was long enough to tantalize but too short to satisfy. He would have kissed her again, but she tugged away to unlock the door.

"Please. I had fun, but I've got to say goodnight." With a haste that was painful to his ego, she slipped inside.

Ben walked to his car, confused and a little angry. What was going on in the lady's head? On previous encounters she'd flirted with him, in the forest she'd been sweetly compassionate, and tonight at the Burger Shack she'd seemed glad enough to spend time with him. Yet the most innocent kiss had sent her scurrying inside like a frightened maiden aunt. Perversely, maddeningly, now that he was interested, she had pulled back.

He turned the key, and the motor revved to life. On the other hand, the thrill of the chase was half the fun.

FROM the darkened window of the dining room, Geena watched Ben drive away. She could still feel a tingle where his lips had brushed hers. If only the evening hadn't had to end so soon. That lightest of light kisses had whet her appetite for more, and she knew she would be concocting sweet dreams of Ben far into the night. Dreams that might have become reality if only her body hadn't rebelled.

At least she knew for sure he was interested, and for now that was enough. Next time Gran had her bridge night, Geena could ask the good doctor to make a house call.

As the red taillights disappeared around the corner her smile faded and Geena put a hand on her midsection. Her stomach felt abnormally distended, hurting even. The Humungoburger had tasted good going down, but she hated the thought of it sitting inside her, releasing calories and fat grams, turning *her* into Humungo Geena.

She ran upstairs to the bathroom, knelt in front of the toilet and put a finger down her throat. Tears squeezed from her scrunched-shut eyes as she leaned forward and threw up her dinner.

THE NEXT MORNING, guilt and depression washed over her. She lay in bed, going over the events of the day before, trying to work out just what had caused the bad feelings. Tod—good. Ben—very good. Dinner...uh-oh, bad. Throwing up... Argh!

It wasn't the first time she'd dealt with overeating that way. But it was the first time she felt she'd let herself down by doing it.

She got out of bed and gazed at her naked body in the mirror. It was as though she was seeing herself for the first time as a stranger might. Every rib was visible, her hip bones protruded and you could hang a hat on her collarbone. Was modeling, was *any* career, worth starving herself for? She'd never questioned that before, but the answer was staring her in the face. *No.*

Her body was her responsibility. Gran was right, she had to stop abusing it. If she truly did like her body, as she'd told Ben, then shouldn't she treat it better? She *was* changing, and her brush with death helped her see with enhanced clarity that her lifestyle was one of the things that needed changing the most.

She put on a dress she'd picked up at her favorite vintage clothing store in New York and dabbed on perfume but decided not to bother with makeup. Downstairs in the kitchen the radio news was on low, and the shelf clock ticked cozily.

"Good morning, Gran," she said, and kissed her grandmother on the temple.

Gran glanced up from her toast and newspaper with a smile. "Erin called and wanted to know if you'd like to take a walk with her and Erik this morning."

"I'd love to. I promised Carrie Wakefield I'd look after Billy for a couple of hours so she could take Tod to the hospital. I'll call Erin in a few minutes."

She turned up the radio in time to hear a news report about the latest events in Guatemala. Following the earthquake, mud slides were claiming hundreds of additional lives. Shivers ran up her arms. But for a difference of a month or so, *Ben* might have been caught in the disaster. She immediately felt badly for all those who were affected.

"Isn't it terrible what's happening in Guatemala?" Gran said, clucking. "I see Dr. Matthews has set up a collection box for donations of clothing and household goods for the earthquake victims. I'm going to start knitting some hats and scarves for the poor souls.''

"That's a nice idea, Gran." Geena went to the fridge and took out the egg carton. "Do you want a boiled egg? I'm making one for myself.''

"I've already eaten, thanks." Gran watched Geena's movements with wide eyes. "Do you feel okay?''

"Except for the news, I feel good." She ran water into a pot and put on the stove, feeling that with those simple actions she was doing something positive for herself. How could she expect anyone else to love her if she didn't love herself? "Really good.''

Despite her intentions, Geena couldn't bring herself to eat the buttered toast she'd made to go with her egg. The crisp golden triangles taunted her from her plate, proving a major change couldn't happen overnight. She ate an orange, instead, and decided to record the food she consumed over the next week and see what the nutritionist said about her improved habits.

Saturday, September 11. Breakfast: Orange, one boiled egg.

Tomorrow, she would eat the toast.

Later that morning, Geena and Erin strolled side by side, each pushing a baby buggy—Geena Billy's and Erin Erik's—through the park by the river.

Broad-leaf maples and oaks were dotted at intervals beside a winding path, their leaves starting to turn color and fall. Children ran, trailing a fluttering red kite in the breeze, and couples strolled, feeding the ducks or sitting on park benches.

It was cool in the shade, giving an edge to the brilliant sunshine, but the babies were bundled up warmly. Geena watched the slight rise and fall of Billy's chest as he slept and fantasized the baby belonged to her. When would it be her turn?

"What's it like being a mother?" Geena asked Erin.

"Wonderful," Erin replied. "I miss work, but not as much as I thought."

"I suppose you'll go back eventually?"

"Yes. The day care is just a few doors away, and I'll be able to see Erik at breaks. At lunch I'll take him down to the fire station to eat with Nick. If he's not at a fire, of course."

"You scored big-time with Nick."

"He's the best. See that bench over there beneath the tree? That's where we first had lunch together." Erin cast her a sly sidelong glance. "Ben Matthews is cute, too. I heard you had dinner with him at the Burger Shack."

"I took Tod over," Geena said noncommittally. "It breaks my heart seeing that poor kid going through the ordeal of chemo. He's really upset now that he's losing his hair.''

"It's great you're spending so much time with him. I never would have thought you'd do something like that—'' Erin broke off abruptly. "Uh-oh, witch alert.''

Geena followed her gaze and groaned. Greta Vogler was heading toward them. "I still haven't finished this week's math assignment,'' Geena muttered to Erin. "She's bound to ask how it's going.''

"Good morning, Geena, Erin,'' Greta said. Clearly it wasn't a good enough morning to make her smile. *Good morning, Miss Vogler,* Geena mentally intoned, hating how her ex-teacher made her feel fifteen again. *Ex*-teacher? She wished. "Hi, Greta.''

"How is your math assignment going?'' Greta asked.

Geena put on a carefree smile. "It's a breeze.''

"Then you'll have it ready for me to look at today.''

"Oh, sure.'' Geena could do confident even when she was shaking in her Molini ankle boots.

Like a predator hunting juicier prey, Greta turned her attention to Erin's baby. "He doesn't look much like his father, does he, poor little chap?'' She clapped a hand over her mouth. "Oh, I'm sorry. I keep forgetting Nick isn't his *real* father.''

"Nick *is* Erik's real father." Erin grated the words out.

"Easy, Erin," Geena said, biting her tongue with difficulty. Erin had been pregnant with her ex-fiancé's child when she'd met Nick. The ex had shirked his responsibilities as a father, but Nick had more than made up for it, embracing Erin's baby as his own.

"I heard Kelly and Max are having problems," Greta went on, not lowering her voice in the slightest. "Not surprising when they wed so young. But it would be awful for those poor children if they split up."

This was too much for Erin. "Mind your own business, Miss Vogler!" she snapped. "You're nothing but a...a dried-up old tea bag."

"Well, I never!" Greta's eyes widened, then narrowed. She clasped her hands in front of her and lifted her pointed chin, just as she used to before giving some poor high school student a detention. "I thought you were a lady, Erin. Guess I was mistaken."

Greta was jealous, Geena realized suddenly. Jealous of Erin and Kelly for their husbands and their children. It didn't excuse her conduct, but it made it easier for Geena to understand. And to try to do as her mother asked.

"Greta," Geena said. "I noticed your hand didn't go up when we called for mature-age models for the fashion show. I really wish you would reconsider."

"Me? Oh, no. No, I don't think so."

"You're well proportioned, and your legs are really nice. Aren't her legs nice, Erin?" Erin uttered a strangled sound, which Geena ignored. "So what do you say, Greta?"

"I'm not glamorous in the least. I'd look a fool." Greta still appeared doubtful, but there was the faintest trace of interest, just enough to encourage Geena.

"I'll give you a complete makeover," Geena said. "It'll be fun."

"A makeover," Greta repeated.

"Excellent," Geena said, as if she'd just agreed. "I'll arrange everything and call you when we're ready."

"All right. But don't forget your algebra assignment. School comes first."

"I'll have plenty of time for everything." She hoped. Algebra was daunting, but undoing twenty years of bad-hair days would be a *real* challenge.

As soon as Greta was out of earshot, Erin shrieked at Geena. "I can't believe you did that."

"I feel sorry for her."

Erin gripped the buggy handle so hard her knuckles were white. "She's a bitter, twisted hag. I don't care what she says about me, but when she's mean about Kelly I want to pop her one."

Geena hesitated. "Erin, you know how, when I collapsed, I went through the tunnel to the light and saw Mom."

Erin's gaze turned wary. "In a dentist's waiting room."

Put baldly, Geena had to admit her story sounded odd, but she plowed on anyway. "Mom told me to be nice to her. To try to forgive her."

Erin stopped walking and stared at her. "You always disliked Greta the most of all of us. So for you to come up with that... Something really happened to you, didn't it?"

Geena nodded, and a tightness in her chest seemed to burst open. Erin believed her.

They walked a little farther without speaking before Erin stopped and raised her face to the cloudless September sky. Moisture shimmered in her gray-blue eyes. "Did Mom...did she mention me?"

"I thought I told you. She said to tell you and Kelly she loved you very much and was really proud of you both."

A tear spilled free and rolled down Erin's cheek. She smiled a wobbly smile. "Yeah?"

"Yeah." Geena put her arms around her sister,

and they clung to each other. After a while, Geena pulled away, wiping her eyes with the heel of her hand.

"Typical, though," Erin said, sniffing, but with a telltale twitching at the corner of her mouth, "that you got to be the one to see her. Mom always liked you best."

Geena punched her lightly. "She did not."

"Did, too."

"Did not."

They laughed and hugged again, and Geena was glad to be home with her sisters once again. They walked to the end of the park, then turned up the Wakefields' street so Geena could drop Billy off. Erin waited at the bottom of the steps while Geena took Billy to the door.

"Tod went to a friend's house, and I got caught up on the housework," Carrie said. "I don't know how to thank you." She looked exhausted, and Geena could smell the lemony scent of cleaning products from the doorway.

"I enjoyed it. Next time, schedule some R and R for yourself. I'm happy to take Billy or Tod, or both if you want. Just give me a call."

"You're an angel." Carrie picked Billy out of the buggy and smiled into his face. "Hi, guy."

Erin teased her as they walked the remaining few

blocks to Gran's. "So, my self-indulgent little sister has become an angel."

"I like doing things for other people," Geena said, a little defensively. "It feels good."

She stopped in front of Erin's car, parked outside the big Victorian home. "I'd suggest you come in, but I've got to do that algebra. Then I told Gran I'd take Edna a ticket to the fashion show."

"Make me some tea, and I'll help you with your algebra," Erin proposed.

"You've got a deal."

CHAPTER EIGHT

"AFTER I HAD my appendix out I was fine for about three months, until my hip started playing up." Wedged behind the ironing board, Edna chatted while she pressed and folded tea towels.

Ben sat at the table with a cup of coffee and nodded to the umpteenth unabridged rendition of Edna's medical history. He'd gone for a jog along the river earlier in the hopes of running into Geena, only to see her in the distance, walking with her sister and pushing a baby buggy. After that, he'd done his shopping, washed his clothes and dropped by Edna's to pick up a box of odds and ends he'd left behind when he moved. Truth was, he'd also come to check up on her. She was pretty fit despite her list of ailments and she had lots of friends to look out for her, but she was no spring chicken. Ben felt better seeing for himself that she was okay. Since Eddie had gone missing, he liked to keep tabs on the people he cared about.

He couldn't concentrate on Edna's sciatica when

the news this morning had told of fresh disasters in the western highlands. He knew his brother would get in touch if he could, but the waiting was so hard. Ben had finally gotten through to International Médicos, but they were unable to tell him of Eddie's whereabouts or confirm whether Eddie was dead or alive. Communication with the village was cut off, and travel to the area was limited to emergency crews. No news was good news, he kept telling himself, but he found that increasingly hard to believe.

There was a knock at the door.

"Can you answer that, Ben?"

Grateful for the diversion, he went to the door.

Geena stood on the step, looking like some 1950s movie star in a peach-colored dress that embraced her slender curves and made her skin glow. He hadn't talked to her since the Burger Shack, and he still felt vaguely chagrined at her unceremonious dismissal of him that evening.

"Hey, there," she said. She had a black canvas tote bag over her shoulder that weighed her down on one side. "Is Edna home?"

"Yes. Come on in." Not for the first time, he wondered how he could be so attracted to a woman so flighty. It almost seemed like a personality defect in himself.

"Hi, Mrs. Thompson," Geena said, following him into the kitchen. "How are you feeling today?"

"Oh, I can't complain. I was just telling Ben I have a twinge of sciatica in my left leg. Would you like a cup of coffee? Some lunch?"

"No, thanks, I've already eaten."

Ben raised an eyebrow.

"An open-face turkey sandwich," Geena said, answering his silent query. "Edna, Gran said you wanted to buy a ticket to our fashion show."

"Just let me get my pocketbook." Edna edged from behind the ironing board and went out of the room.

Idly, Ben reached for the book of tickets Geena had laid on the round wooden table and glanced at the details. "So this is your date for the seventeenth. Are you modeling?"

She dropped her tote bag with a clunk to the floor. "I can handle it," she said, a little defensively.

"It's not that. Don't you ever think you'd like to do something less—" He broke off. Feeling scornful of Geena and her ilk was easy when she was just a face in a newspaper, but now he knew her a little. She was a human being, with strengths and weaknesses—and feelings.

"Less what?" Her expression turned wary, as if she'd guessed where this was going.

"Nothing."

"Less superficial?"

He ran a hand through his hair. "You've got to admit, the money women spend on clothes could be used for more worthwhile causes. The cost of one designer dress would feed a kid in Guatemala for a year." When he thought of his brother toiling away for next to nothing to help people who had even less...

Hurt sparked in her deep blue eyes, but her answer was offhand. "It's a job, okay? We can't all be doctors or...or rocket scientists."

"You don't have to be a rocket scientist to do something worthwhile."

"I know that." She inspected her nails, maddeningly unconcerned.

"Here you go," Edna said, coming into the room, digging bills out of her purse. "I'll take two tickets. My sister from Yakima is visiting next month. What's the fashion show in aid of, Geena?"

"The ladies' auxiliary is raising money for the Guatemala Earthquake Relief Fund."

Ben stared at her. "You could have told me that before I ran off at the mouth."

"And miss the benefit of your expert opinion?"

"No one's mentioned this fund to me," Ben said, still nonplussed.

"I think Mabel's waiting to see if we pull it off."

Edna cleared her throat. "I saw in the *Hainesville Herald* that the snow geese have arrived at the waterfowl refuge on their way south. It's a lovely day outside."

"I have to go," Geena said, putting away the ticket book and gathering her bag. "Thanks for supporting the fashion show, Mrs. Thompson. I'll let myself out." She barely glanced at Ben as the door shut behind her.

"If you'll excuse me, Edna," Ben said. "I have to leave, too." He started after Geena, only to pull up short. "Damn. My box of things."

"You can get it later," Edna said. "Hurry now, or she'll be halfway down the street on those long legs of hers."

Ben caught up to Geena at the corner. Chin high, she looked straight ahead and ignored him. Not knowing what to say, he walked beside her. "Where are you going?"

She slanted him a narrow-eyed look. "To return some library books, and then I have to drop off an assign— I have to visit someone."

"Feel like a walk when you're done? See the snow geese?"

"Sorry, I'm busy."

"Have to wash your hair?"

She glared at him. "I washed it this morning."

"Sorry, I'm teasing. You look lovely, as usual. I saw you and your sister this morning," he added casually. "Whose baby was that you were walking?"

"Carrie Wakefield's. She needed some time."

"That was nice of you. You know, you can get scoliosis of the spine from carrying a heavy load on one shoulder. Let me help you." He tried to lift her bag. She jerked her arm away, and the bag tipped, spilling books onto the sidewalk.

"Now look what you've done." She seemed unduly upset, grabbing frantically for her books.

"Sorry." He crouched to help her and picked up a thick hardback text. *"Algebra?"*

"Give me that. It's…it's my niece's. I'm returning it for her." She took the book roughly from his hand and shoved it into the tote bag.

Ben spotted one she'd missed lying in the grass near the sidewalk and picked it up. The cover depicted a woman in a flowing white gown reaching for a bright light. *"Transformed by the Light,"* he said. "What's this about?"

"Nothing," she said, trying to tug it away from him.

Intrigued, he twisted away from her so he could read the back-cover blurb. "A study of people who have had near-death experiences." He glanced over his shoulder at her. "Are you still hung up on this near-death thing?"

She snatched the book from him and shoved it into her bag. "It's not a hang-up. After reading of other people's experiences so similar to mine, I'm more convinced than ever that it's real. So don't tell me I'm talking rubbish."

"I wouldn't dare, but there are facts you should be aware of." He leaned against a tree and crossed his arms over his chest. "I recently read an account of a study on the effect of G force on fighter pilots. When the pilots are subjected to acceleration, blood drains from their brain. Just before they lose consciousness, they experience sensations similar to those claimed by people with near-death experiences—a tunneling of vision and a bright light. Apparently, while the brain is starved for oxygen, the neurons that deal with vision fire at random, creating the sensation of bright light. Because more neurons are at the center of our visual field and fewer are at the edges, you get a tunneling effect."

She stared at him, hands planted on her slender hips. "That proves nothing. My near death was the most beautiful experience I've ever had."

"That's not surprising," Ben said. "In times of great stress, the brain releases opiate-like substances to relieve anxiety. These produce hallucinations in parts of the brain that deal with memories and emotions. The pilots in the study experienced euphoria just before they blacked out.''

Geena laughed in disbelief and pretended to tear out her hair. ''I don't care what the studies say. I didn't just feel euphoria—I felt *love*.''

''Love is the biggest emotional high, is it not?'' Ben said, clinching his argument.

She shook her head. ''You don't understand.''

''I'm trying to help *you* understand. All these so-called paranormal incidents can be explained scientifically.''

She slung her bag over her shoulder. ''Science doesn't have all the answers, Ben Matthews. Open your mind. You might be surprised at what flows in.''

And then she was gone, hurrying around the corner. Ben gazed after her, shaking his head. Just when he thought he was beginning to know her, just when they were beginning to connect, some damn thing would blow up in their faces. If it wasn't her modeling, it was her near-death experience. Baby-sitting for a relative stranger, believing in the paranormal...*algebra?*

Who the hell was Geena Hanson, anyway?

DAMN! Why couldn't he have caught her reading *War and Peace?* Not that she'd ever even cracked *that*

doorstop of a book. Oh, God, and he'd seen her algebra text! If he ever figured out why she was studying high school math she'd just die.

Her embarrassment flipped to anger as she recalled
his lecture on the real explanation for her near-death
experience. Lifting her chin, she drew her tote bag
over her shoulder. *You can't convince a skeptic,* she
told herself, ignoring the little voice that insisted Ben
was different. That he should have understood, or at
least accepted.

He always seemed to comment on her looks,
whether it was to knock her profession and its emphasis on image or to tell her she was lovely. What
would happen when her face grew old and wrinkled
and lost its appeal? No matter how many beauty
treatments she undertook or how rigorously she
watched her diet, she would age. Just like everyone
else. Who would want her then? Not the men she
met at Cannes or Saint Moritz. They would go on to
someone younger, someone new.

Ben was the kind of man who would love a
woman for who she was inside. But he didn't take
Geena seriously. If only he could see beyond the superficial to the real Geena. Why couldn't he notice
some of her positive qualities? She was beginning to
realize Mom was right; she did have a talent for help-

ing people. As a doctor, Ben should be tuned in to that sort of thing.

By the time she got to Greta's house, she'd almost convinced herself that Ben's opinion didn't matter to her. She forgot all about Ben when Greta opened the door holding a Barbie doll. Malibu Barbie.

Greta folded the doll protectively between her hands. "Don't stand there. Come in."

"I just came to drop off my algebra assignment...."

But Greta had already disappeared into a room to the left of the foyer. Geena followed, intensely curious. As a teenager, going into a teacher's house would have been unthinkable; even now, it was pretty mind-blowing.

She stepped into the living room and blinked. On the far wall was a glass-fronted cabinet displaying shelf upon shelf of Barbie dolls. Mesmerized, Geena walked to the cabinet. A representative of every Barbie doll ever made seemed to be in that case—Cowboy Barbie, Nurse Barbie, Firefighter Barbie—they were all there. The dolls were lined up four and five deep, jostling each other with their wide shoulders, each jabbing the one in front with her pointy breasts.

"Wow," she breathed, turning to Greta. "Did you collect all these?"

"I started when I was nine and I've never

stopped," Greta said from her seat by the coffee table. She had five or six Barbies out and was packing them into a Barbie carrying case. "You're a little late, so I don't have much time right now. I'm on my way to a meeting of the Barbie Club. I'm newly elected president of my chapter," she added with a trace of pride.

Geena couldn't suppress at smile. "The Barbie Club?"

"I hope you're not laughing," Greta said sharply. "Barbies are big business, you know. In mint condition they can sell for up to ten thousand dollars."

"Is that why you do it? As an investment?"

Greta stroked the long black hair of the Barbie in her hand, and her face softened. "No one does it just for the money."

Geena perused the faces and costumes of the dolls in the cabinet. One, wearing black horn-rims and a white coat, looked familiar. "I had a Dr. Barbie just like this when I was a kid."

Greta seemed to know exactly which doll she meant. "I got her from a church rummage sale...oh, I guess it was back in 1982."

Geena did a quick mental calculation. "That would have been about the time I last remember seeing mine. I always wondered what happened to Dr. Barbie." She sighed. "I guess Gran got rid of her when I stopped playing with dolls. Who knows, maybe this was mine.''

There was silence behind her, and she turned to see Greta watching her anxiously. ''You don't want her back, do you?''

''Heavens, no.'' Geena hastened to assure her and moved to the coffee table. ''What are these?''

''They're from a line Mattel brought out last year called the fashion model collection. They're made from a new vinyl substance. Aren't they beautiful?''

''Uh, sure,'' Geena said, a little uncomfortable with the concept. She reached into her tote bag. ''I finished my algebra. I had a little help with some of the equations.''

''That's fine, as long as you understand how you got the answer.'' Greta glanced over the set of problems. ''Very good.''

She rose, went to a rolltop desk in the corner of the room and took a sheet of paper from a stack. ''Here are some trigonometry problems. See how you do with these. If you have trouble, come to me.''

''Thanks. I'll go and let you get to your meeting.''

Greta walked her to the door. ''I gave you that Dr. Barbie shortly after your parents died.''

Geena stared. ''I didn't know that.''

''I felt so badly for you girls. You were only three,

too young for a Barbie, really, but I gave your sisters each one and thought you'd want the same.''

Had the Barbie dolls been a guilt offering for maligning her father? ''Why should you feel badly?''

Say it, Greta. Say, ''I'm sorry.''

Greta suddenly looked flustered, as though she'd revealed too much. ''Their death was a tragedy. Anyone would feel sad for three orphaned girls.''

''You know, Greta, my father wasn't drunk that night. He swerved to avoid a dog.''

Greta's face went white. ''How do you know? Who told you?''

Despite her good intentions, Geena lashed out with long-held grief and resentment. ''You shouldn't have spread rumors about my father. It wasn't right.''

Greta's face closed, and she stepped back from the doorway. ''I have to get ready for my meeting.''

Shoulders slumping, Geena turned to go. What did she expect from Greta anyway—a public apology?

At the steps she paused and, with great difficulty, said, ''Thanks for the Barbie...back then. It was a nice thing to do.''

To her surprise, Greta's eyes shimmered moistly. ''Go on. Go on with you. You'll make me late.''

''How is next Thursday after school for your makeover?'' Geena said.

''Make it the following Friday. I can take a half

day off then. But if you're buttering me up, you're wasting your time,'' Greta added sharply. ''I have nothing to do with the final GED exam.''

Geena gave up and said a terse goodbye. Thank goodness she wasn't after sainthood—she'd be lucky if she managed forgiveness.

SATURDAY MORNING Ben made the rounds at the Fernwood Aged Care Facility. Finished with his patients, he paused to talk to the head nurse, his voice slightly raised over the lively conversation going on next door in the common room.

''Confine Mr. Rankin to bed with his leg elevated and apply warm compresses,'' he said. ''I'll make arrangements with the hospital for some tests—'' Ben broke off at the sound of familiar laughter. Only one person he knew laughed like that.

It wasn't a feminine tinkle or a ladylike trill but a full-throated guffaw—a laugh that made him instinctively want to smile, even though he was discussing Mr. Rankin's thrombosis.

''I'm sorry if the noise is disturbing you, Dr. Matthews,'' Nurse Wells said, anxiously fingering her pendant watch. ''Geena Hanson came in to visit one of her grandmother's friends, and now she has a whole crowd of ladies gathered around her. I'm afraid she's got them all excited. I'll put a stop to it at once.''

''No, please don't,'' Ben said, holding up a hand. ''A bit of excitement might be just what they need.''

Taking a couple of steps, he peered around the open door into the spacious common room. Couches and a TV occupied one corner, a small exercise floor with a full wall of mirrors took up another, and in the open center Geena held court, surrounded by a cluster of six or seven elderly women in chairs or wheelchairs. They all looked as though they were having a whale of a good time, no one more so than Geena. The unexpectedness of seeing her made his heart beat faster. His conscience was pricking him over her. He was afraid he'd been unnecessarily scathing over her near-death experience. He didn't know why he should take her beliefs so personally.

Nurse Wells bustled past Ben in spite of his admonition to leave them alone and announced loudly, ''It's almost time for lunch, ladies.''

Disappointed murmurs rose from the group, but they started to break up. As Ben watched Geena help the women put away chairs, a crazy idea took root in his brain. What if she gave up modeling to work in palliative care or something similar? She was so at ease with people, so full of genuine warmth for others, she would be a fantastic carer. *Plus,* he thought, giving in to fantasy, such a career would fit in with his life as a small-town doctor.

Then Ben saw her pass the mirror and automatically check her hair, her dress, her look. He would like to think it was a typically feminine response to his presence, but he was afraid it went deeper—or shallower, depending on how he looked at it. As a professional model she was first and foremost conscious of her image. Even her graceful progress across the room was a carefully cultivated product of her training. And why would anyone, no matter how much enjoyment was gained helping people, give up a lucrative, glamorous career for one of hard work, high stress and low pay?

"Hello, Ben," she said, coolly. She would have slipped past him with a perfunctory nod had he not done an about-face and walked with her out of the building.

"I'm surprised to see you here," he said. "I wouldn't have thought you'd spend your Saturday morning entertaining the elderly."

She tossed him a saucy smile. "Just working on my Brownie points." His gaze must have revealed his complete lack of understanding, because she sighed. "Maybe they were entertaining *me*. I got as much enjoyment out of my visit with the ladies as I hope they did."

"That would certainly appear to be the case." He hesitated. "Have you ever thought of working with the elderly?"

She laughed, reverting to flippancy. "This can't be work. It's too much fun. Besides, I'm not *qualified*."

That shut him up until they reached his car. His thoughts and feelings were confused where Geena was concerned. He, who always knew his own mind and heart. "Can I give you a lift somewhere?"

"No, thanks. I'm walking." But she didn't immediately move off, as though, in spite of her restless energy, she was waiting for him to say something.

He might as well get it over with. Ben's gaze drifted from the pine grove behind the aged care facility to the totem pole erected out front to the weeds growing through a crack in the pavement. Finally, he looked her in the eye. "I apologize if I offended you the other day."

She crossed her arms and leaned against his car. "So you concede there's such a thing as a near-death experience?"

"Oh, I wouldn't go that far."

She gave a short laugh. "Goodbye, Ben." And turned to walk away.

"Geena…" He fished a flat square plastic case out of his pocket and handed it to her. "I was going to stop by your house later. This is for you. I thought you might like it.''

The CD he'd given her was a compilation of love songs; in the number one spot was the ballad Tod had chosen on the jukebox at the Burger Shack. Ben had only meant it as a friendly gesture, but all at once he regretted his choice. She might read more into his gift than he cared to admit.

Amazingly, she looked so touched he was afraid she might cry. ''Thank you. I—''

''Snow geese,'' he said in a hurry, not letting her finish. ''Saturday afternoon.'' Lest she think he meant it as a romantic tryst—did he?—he added, ''Bring Tod.''

''He'd like that.'' She hesitated. ''I will, too.''

Briefly, his fingers found hers, linked, squeezed and parted. Geena smiled into his eyes and turned to walk swiftly away. Ben chuckled, suddenly restored to good humor and easy conscience. He and Geena were friends again. Maybe more than friends.

CHAPTER NINE

"TOD'LL BE OUT in a minute, he's just getting his jacket on," Carrie told Geena when she went to pick him up. "He's so excited about the snow geese." She paused and went on, a tremor in her voice, "I'd hoped that last run of chemo would put him in remission, but his white blood cell count is still high. Although the doctors don't say anything to him, Tod can tell things aren't good."

Geena impulsively squeezed Carrie's hand. "Are you sure he's up to a walk?"

"I borrowed a wheelchair from the hospital in case he can't go the whole way." Billy came toddling around the corner in a diaper and T-shirt, one hand on the wall for support, and Carrie bent to scoop him into her arms. "If you don't mind pushing him when he gets tired, that is."

"Of course not. The trails at the waterfowl refuge are gravel, but they're hard packed, and we shouldn't have a problem."

"Mom, I can't get the zipper done up," Tod said

as he emerged from his room. He glanced down the hall, and his face lit up. "Hi, Geena!"

"Hey, there, Mr. Buster," she said cheerily. "Let me get that zipper for you." Quelling her shock at how pale and thin he looked, she knelt in front of him to free the zipper. Beneath the loose sleeve she could see bruises on his forearm from where the drip had been inserted. "How are you? Been eating your Brussels sprouts?"

Tod made a face and spoke behind his hand in a theatrical whisper. "Mom found something worse—spinach!"

"I love spinach. Makes you strong, like Popeye. Boy, this zipper is really stuck."

"Popeye's nothing. You should see the Terminator."

"Have *you* seen the Terminator?"

Carrie shook her head. "No, and he's not going to."

"I saw the previews on TV." Tod studied her with a puzzled frown. "You look different. Fatter."

"Nice guy!" she said, laughing. The zipper went up, and she got to her feet. "You'll never get a girlfriend with that kind of flattery."

"Yuck! I don't want a girlfriend." He tucked his hand in hers. "Except maybe you."

Geena's heart gave a little lurch. *Please God, don't let anything happen to this child.*

"Did you know that thirty-five hundred tons of cosmic dust falls on the earth every year?" Tod added.

"I had no idea. Maybe Ben knows about cosmic dust," she said, blinking. "I think I heard his car pull up."

"Quick, more birdseed, Dr. Ben, or they'll eat *me* next." Excitement and fresh air colored Tod's pale cheeks, and he laughed, lifting his empty hands away from the dozens of quacking mallards that surrounded him.

"Be careful they don't bite your fingers." Ben handed him the small sack of seed they'd bought at the visitors' center and kept a supportive hand on the boy's back to make sure Tod didn't get knocked off his feet by the sheer numbers of waterfowl. He glanced at Geena, throwing seed a little way off, trying to lure some of the ducks away from Tod.

She met his gaze, and his heart lifted at the sight of her smile. Her red leather jacket with its beads and braiding added color to the day. Even the gum boots he'd brought for her, knowing she'd probably wear fashionable, impractical footwear, couldn't detract from her aura of glamour.

"Just call me Cinderella," she'd murmured humorously as he'd knelt before her at the picnic table, guiding her long, narrow foot into a boot.

"Guess that makes me your prince," he'd said, and performed a mock bow. "You look beautiful, milady."

She rewarded him with her full-throated laugh. "Prince Charming, you have such a way with words."

Obviously, she'd heard all the compliments a million times before, but she couldn't know how much he meant his. When he was with her, he forgot his worry over Eddie, his concern for Tod. She had a child's knack of being fully in the present. Not that she was childish or even childlike. Though her body was waif-thin, her deep blue eyes held a woman's mystique. Yet it still bothered him that he was so attracted to her. The last person he wanted for a partner was a fashion plate, no matter how caring and kind she was to a little boy.

Enjoy the moment. Quit looking for absolutes.

Playfully, he threw a handful of seed at Geena's feet, then regretted it when a gaggle of Canada geese lumbered out of the water, dispersing the ducks, and began to peck aggressively at her knees.

"Time to move on," Ben said, emptying the contents of the sack on the ground. Shielding Tod with his body, he took Geena's hand and strode through the milling birds while they pecked frenziedly at the scattered seed.

"Have we got seed left for the snow geese?" Tod asked, as they moved down a trail bounded on one side by a thick hedge of alder and thimbleberry and on the other by a series of lagoons.

"Three bags full, sir," Ben replied, patting the bulging pockets of his navy wool bomber jacket. They were walking along the top of a dike, he realized, catching glimpses through the hedge of half-flooded pasture land at a lower elevation. Geena's slim, soft hand felt good wrapped in his.

"Are you sure you don't want to bring the wheel-chair?" Geena peered around Ben to ask Tod. "Your mom was worried you might get tired."

Tod's small chin rose. "Mom worries too much."

Ben squeezed Geena's hand to reassure her. "We won't go too far." He glanced ahead a half a mile to a wooden structure rising from the trees. "But let's see if we can make it to the observation tower."

He reined in his long stride and instinctive desire to get where he was going, knowing they had to stroll for Tod's sake. But he was amused that Geena, even more than Tod, was forever stopping to look at a plant or insect along the path.

"Did you ever think about becoming a biologist?" he asked.

"You seem determined to get me out of modeling and into another line of work," she said with a laugh, then crouched to turn her rapt gaze to the iridescent green back of a large beetle. "I'm not interested in Latin names or how an insect breathes. Look, Tod, his little feelers are waving at you." To Ben, she added, "I'm just fascinated by all the weird and wonderful forms that life comes in. It seems so...miraculous." She blushed, as though embarrassed by her enthusiasm.

Again he wondered, who *was* this woman? How could she be captivated by beetles and still care what color lipstick was in this season? "Have you always been interested in flora and fauna?"

"No." She rose, smoothing the creases out of her black pants. "Only since...Milan."

In other words, since her near-death experience. This week he'd researched more articles on the subject in medical and scientific journals, but nothing he'd read suggested the phenomenon was anything other than the biochemical response of a body deprived of life-giving oxygen. *She* believed as fervently as another might believe in religion. Today he would avoid the subject.

"I'm going to take him home. Can I?" Tod held the beetle in his cupped hands, glancing from Ben to Geena. "I'll train him like I trained Arnie."

''That would be all right for a little while,'' Ben said. ''As long as you keep him in a container with the things he likes—grass, leaves, dirt.''

''Cool.'' Tod's eyes lit.

''You'll have to check with your mom when you get home,'' Geena warned, handing him a crumpled birdseed sack from her pocket to carry the beetle in. ''What she says goes.''

''Okay,'' Tod said happily. He put the beetle in the sack and went ahead, pausing now and then to pick up a choice clump of leaves for his beetle. Ben and Geena followed more slowly.

As if by mutual agreement, they halted before a bend in the path. Tod was momentarily out of sight, but they could hear him up ahead, chattering happily to his beetle.

A gust of wind blew Geena's hair across her eyes. Ben reached out to brush it away, and his hand lingered to stroke her cheek. ''I bought a ticket to your fashion show,'' he confessed.

She smiled and teased, ''I'm surprised at you.''

''It's for a good cause. And to tell you the truth, I'm looking forward to watching you perform.''

She turned her face into his hand, and he felt her lips press into his palm. Heat shot through his body as the fantasies and desires of countless daydreams coalesced into the touch of her lips.

"What are we going to do?" he whispered, breathing in her sweetly spicy scent. "We're so different."

She lifted her mouth to his as he drew her close. "What we're doing now seems pretty good."

Ben felt his hunger rise as he pressed against her soft lips. She was wrong, so wrong for him, but she tasted like light and joy and sheer happiness. With a moan, he gathered her into his arms and deepened the kiss. He'd wanted to do this since the first time she'd walked into his office, sassy and sultry and exquisitely feminine.

"Geena, Dr. Matthews, come quickly," Tod called. "The snow geese."

With a regretful smile, Geena pulled away. As Ben's hands slid from her waist, his doctor's instinct registered a change in her. *Had she gained weight?* He didn't dare ask, not right after he'd touched her not as a doctor but as a man.

Geena ran ahead, stopping beside Tod to peer through a gap in the hedge. She glanced at Ben. "It *is* them! Come on."

Ben leaned over Geena's shoulder to look, too conscious of her nearness to focus very clearly on the hundreds of big snow-white birds feeding in the soggy pasture below the dike. Beyond the geese lay the broad mouth of the river, and beyond that the ocean shimmered on the horizon.

"Can we go down there and see them up close?" Tod said, eagerly.

"Seems pretty wet, and we might scare them away." Ben nodded to the observation tower. "If we climb up there and look through my binoculars, we'll have a good view."

Easier said than done, Ben realized halfway up the steep wooden steps. Tod had already expended much of his limited energy on the walk and had to rest every few minutes. His breath came in shallow pants, and fierce color burned in two spots on his otherwise white face.

"We can probably see just as well from below," Geena suggested, her anxious gaze seeking support from Ben.

"We could," Ben said, angry with himself for not foreseeing this and stopping Tod before he'd experienced failure and weakness. Angrier still at a disease that was robbing the boy of his childhood, perhaps cutting his life unnaturally short. He stopped his thoughts from going in that direction—death was never an option—and deliberately gentled his tone. "What do you say, Tod?"

"I can make it, Dr. Ben. Please. I want to see the snow geese." Tod was biting his bottom lip in an effort not to cry, whether from pain and exhaustion or frustration, Ben couldn't tell.

Ben moved up the steps until he was alongside Tod. "Climb on my back, son. I'll take you the rest of the way."

Tod clambered onto Ben's back and wrapped his arms around Ben's neck. The boy was light, *too* light, and in a matter of moments, they were at the top of the tower. Geena helped Tod slide down and gave the boy a hug and a kiss, which seemed to embarrass and please him in equal measure.

"Look, Tod," Ben said, pointing out the sights. "To the east is Hainesville. I think I can see your house. Your mom's in the yard, waving." Tod giggled and waved at the rooftops amid the trees. Ben turned him ninety degrees. "There's Simcoe, and there to the north are the mountains—"

"The Olympic Mountains," Geena elaborated.

"What's out there?" Tod asked, pointing west to the seemingly boundless ocean.

"That's the Pacific Ocean. It extends west all the way to Hawaii and Japan and south to Australia."

"When I grow up, I'm going to sail across it," Tod declared, his eyes shining. Then his face clouded, and he went quiet.

Ben straightened, struggling to control the sudden thickness in his throat. The boy reminded him of

Eddie, always making big plans. Ben pulled his binoculars from his pocket and wrapped Tod's small hands around them. "Look through these. Tell me what the snow geese are doing."

He showed Tod how to focus and then turned to lean over the rail facing the mountains. As a doctor he knew he shouldn't get emotionally involved with Tod, but how could he *not?*

Thank God for Geena. She took over, chatting about the geese to Tod, making everything seem normal.

Then he heard Tod say, "Am I going to die?"

He swiveled to see Tod's small upturned face, frowning but waiting trustingly for Geena's answer. Ben was about to intervene, to talk to Tod about percentages, the efficacy of various treatments and the likelihood of remission, when Geena laid a hand on Tod's head and smiled into his eyes.

"No, Tod, you're not going to die," she said with calm authority. "It's not your time."

Ben stared, speechless and appalled. He couldn't believe she'd said that.

Geena's pronouncement had a quite different effect on Tod. His face relaxed, and the tiny lines between his brow smoothed. His mouth, always a cross between that of an imp and a cherub, lifted in a beatific smile. "Good."

"We've got to go," Ben said more roughly than he'd intended, and guided Tod to the ladder.

"Aw," Tod complained, but his protest seemed more a matter of form than a real disinclination to leave. His shoulders drooped; his feet dragged. He was tired.

All the way to Tod's house, Ben didn't trust himself to look at Geena. While Tod chattered on happily about the snow geese, Ben felt Geena's puzzled gaze on him. If she didn't know what was wrong, he was going to tell her—as soon as Tod was out of earshot. With Tod safely in his house, Ben drove around the corner and parked.

Geena glanced around. "Why did you stop here?"

He turned in his seat to face her, one arm over the steering wheel, one along the back of the seat. "How could you say to Tod that it's not his time to die?"

"Pardon?" She leaned against the door and stared at him.

"You heard me. Do you have any idea how much damage you can do by giving Tod a false sense of security?"

She shook her head, bewildered. "He's only a little boy. He needs to feel safe."

Ben thumped the steering wheel. "This is a world where earthquakes and floods can sweep away a whole village, where disease can strike an innocent child without warning. *There is no such thing as safe.*''

''Where's the harm?'' she demanded, recovering herself to lean forward and jab him in the chest with a long nail. ''You're upset about your brother, understandably so, but don't extend that to Tod.''

''Do *you* know what his chances are, medically speaking?'' He saw something flicker in her eyes and knew with bitter triumph he'd scored a point. ''Tod needs to *fight* his illness, not sit back and wait for divine intervention.''

''You know that's not what I meant.''

''Do I? You've tried to convince me you've seen God.''

''I doubt Tod thinks of it in those terms.'' For the first time, she sounded uncertain.

''He may not articulate it as such, but you can bet the idea is percolating in his head. You need to let Tod know you don't have a direct line to the Almighty.''

Geena crossed her arms over her chest, clearly pushed too far by his last remark. ''You're blowing this out of proportion. I've done nothing wrong, and I'm not taking back a word.''

Ben let out a frustrated breath. ''Don't say anything like that to him again. Maybe he'll forget.''

"I'm not going to promise anything. If he wants to talk about death, I think he should be allowed to."

"Yes, but with counselors who know what they're doing."

The arrow found its mark. She threw him a sharp glance full of hurt before turning away. "Take me home, please," she said, and he could hear tears thickening her words.

Feeling as though he'd been in a brawl, Ben drove through the quiet streets to the big white Victorian house on the corner. Ruth Hanson was in the yard, pruning her roses, when Ben pulled up. Geena didn't wait for him to open her door. With a muttered good-bye, she got out and hurried through the low gate in the picket fence. Ruth spoke to her, received a brief answer, then after an uncertain glance at Ben, followed Geena inside the house.

She was in the wrong; he had no doubt about that. But being right didn't make him happy.

"I'VE CHANGED my mind," Greta stated defiantly from her couch. "I'm not going in the fashion show."

"What! Why not?" Geena exclaimed in dismay.

"I just don't want to," Greta said like an obstinate child.

"But I've got everything arranged. The hairstylist

shuffled appointments to fit you in. The clothing store is assembling a group of outfits for you to try on. This is your big chance to break out of the fashion rut you've been trapped in for the past twenty years.''

''The inner self is more important than external appearances,'' Greta said primly.

That Geena agreed didn't prevent her from being annoyed. She and the others had gone to a lot of trouble to plan and execute Greta's makeover. ''External appearances *reflect* the inner person,'' she snapped. ''If you back out now you are a dried-up old maid from your moldy tweed right through to your marrow.''

Greta's face blanched. ''If that's what you think of me, I don't know why you bothered in the first place.''

Geena groaned with instant regret. That was too harsh even for Greta. ''I'm sorry. That was a horrible, horrible thing to say. But honestly, Greta. Is this—'' she gestured to Greta's ancient shapeless cardigan ''—who you really are? You can't sit around waiting for people to recognize your true worth. You've got to strut your stuff. Show the world you like yourself by sprucing yourself up. Let others know you're a force to be reckoned with. Out with the plain and dowdy and in with the bold and beautiful!''

Greta froze into silence. Her mouth was pinched, her eyes tight; her whole face seemed to shrink inward like the dried head of an apple doll.

Geena threw her hands up. ''Okay, Greta. Forget it. You don't have to do anything you're not comfortable with. I'll see you later.''

Geena was closing the door behind her when she heard a sound like crying. She paused. She heard it again and turned. Greta was sitting on her chair, feet primly together, hands folded on her lap, tears running down her face.

Greta sniffed and looked at Geena with misery in her eyes. ''I'll do it. I'll do the show. Just tell me how to look good.''

Geena smiled. ''I promise you will look so good your neighbors won't know you.''

Twenty minutes later Greta was ensconced in a chair at the beauty salon.

''What are we having done today?'' Hairstylist Wendy Harmon, black clad and rake thin, combed her fingers through Greta's carefully arranged iron-gray coif, unraveling the curls and eliciting an outraged gasp from the vice principal.

''Just a trim,'' Greta insisted, trying to pat her hair into place.

"The works," Geena stated, equally firmly, staring down her ex-teacher in the mirror of Wendy's hair salon. "Give her a modern cut, kind of high in the back, full in the front. Then a nice dark all-over color to go with her eyes."

"Brunet with red highlights?" Wendy suggested.

"Perfect." Geena noticed Greta's silent gape through the mirror and smiled reassuringly. "Sit back and relax, Greta. *I'm* in charge now."

Two hours later, Greta sat in stony silence as Wendy scrunch-dried Greta's hair into a tangle of curls that framed and softened her angular face. "You've got fantastic hair," Wendy said, slicking on styling products in strategic places. "It's so thick and wonderfully curly."

Geena watched from another chair, glancing up now and then as she painted her nails pale apricot. With the gray covered and the glint of red brightening the dark brown, Geena thought Greta looked fully ten years younger, and said so.

"*I* don't even know me," Greta said at last.

"But do you like it?"

"I don't know."

With a final brush of Greta's exposed neck, Wendy unwrapped the cape with a flourish. "Ta-da."

"Thanks, Wendy," Geena said. "She looks fantastic."

"Hmph," Greta mumbled noncommittally. She climbed out of the chair, still casting suspicious glances into the mirror as if she couldn't quite believe that was her. She opened her purse. "How much is this costing me?"

"Not a thing," Geena said, nudging her aside and slapping down her credit card. "My idea, my treat." When Greta started to protest, she added, "Please accept my thanks for helping me with—" her eyes flicked to Wendy "—you know."

"No, I don't know," Greta said, maddeningly obtuse.

"Never mind. Why don't you wait outside. I'll be right with you." Geena scribbled her signature at the bottom of the credit card slip and hurried after Greta, taking her arm before she could get in the car. "We're not finished, Greta."

"What now?" Greta demanded. "You've already changed me beyond recognition."

Beneath Greta's belligerent expression, Geena detected fear. "Would that be so bad? No, don't answer that. It takes time to get used to change. You need new clothes to go with your new hairdo," Geena said, leading her down the street to Briony's Women's Wear.

Greta balked. "I'm not buying a whole new wardrobe and I'm not letting you pay for it, either."

"Models are often gifted the clothes they model," Geena said, thinking fast. "I told Briony about your makeover, and she agreed to give you a substantial discount because the publicity will compensate for lost revenue." She hoped she could make a deal to pay the extra for the clothes without Greta knowing. She wasn't quite sure why she was going to so much trouble for Greta, only that it had something to do with honoring her mother and something to do with a Dr. Barbie doll given to a small child in mourning.

"Well, all right," Greta agreed ungraciously. "As long as you don't dress this piece of mutton up as lamb."

"Greta, Greta," Geena remonstrated gently. "Briony has stylish, contemporary fashions for the mature figure. No one wants or expects you to look like a twenty-year-old."

Indeed, by the time Briony and Geena had finished with her, Greta looked like a very attractive forty-something rather than the fifty-something Geena suspected she was. The sleek modern style of Greta's new outfit flattered her figure and complimented her coloring.

Goodness knows what Greta thought. The older woman stood in front of the mirror turning this way and that, looking as if she was about to cry. "It's...it's..."

Geena took in a long breath. She was exhausted after jollying Greta along all day, and if her ex-teacher said one more nasty word she was going to blow a fuse. "It's *what*, Greta?"

"It's unbelievable. I'm...almost beautiful."

Geena exhaled hard and had to blink. "Not *almost*, you silly! You're positively stunning. You've been hiding your light under a bushel all these years."

Geena did a deal with Briony while Greta got her old clothes from the changing room, and soon they were out the door, loaded down with bags.

"Now what?" Greta asked with new enthusiasm. "I'm ready for anything."

Geena smiled. "I'm afraid that's all for now. It's five-thirty. All the stores are shutting for the day."

"Look at me." Greta gave a self-deprecating laugh. "All dressed up and nowhere to go."

"Let's go for coffee," Geena said on impulse. "I'm expected at Kelly's for dinner, but I can be a little late."

Greta brightened immediately, then made a daring suggestion. "Or something stronger? A cocktail at the hotel?"

"Oh, Greta, you naughty thing." Laughing, Geena opened the trunk of her car and stowed the bags in-

side. "Let's walk. You need to show off a little."
Greta started to protest, and Geena silenced her.
"There's no harm in that."

Down the block, they ran into Orville Johannson
as he was locking up his barbershop. "Hi, Geena."
He glanced at Greta and did a double take. "Greta
Vogler? Is that you? You look..." He trailed off, at
a loss for words, then swallowed, still staring. "Nice.
You look really nice."

Geena thought he could have done better than that,
but Greta blushed as if he'd pronounced her a queen.
"Thank you, Orville. Geena's given me a makeover."

"Highly successful, if I may say so," Orville said
gallantly, recovering himself. "Where are you ladies
off to on this fine evening?"

Greta floundered, but Geena immediately invited
him to the hotel for a drink with them.

"Well, now, I don't mind if I do." Orville got in
step beside Greta.

"Oh, look, there's Dr. Matthews," Greta said, and
Geena's heart dropped. Ahead on the street, Ben
came out of Blackwell's Drugstore.

He was about to get into his black Saab when he
spotted them and hesitated. Geena's footsteps faltered. After their last encounter she dreaded another
meeting, even as she longed to make up. She sus-

pected Ben was too principled to back down, and she knew she was too stubborn to admit any wrongdoing.

And why should she? she thought, picking up her pace. She'd spoken out of love for Tod, and how could that be wrong?

"Dr. Matthews," Greta called gaily. "We're all going to the hotel for a cocktail. Will you join us?"

CHAPTER TEN

"MISS VOGLER?" Ben said. "I never would have recognized you. You look extraordinarily lovely today."

"Thanks to Geena." Greta beamed and gingerly touched her new hairstyle. "She's a miracle worker."

"I did nothing," Geena protested.

"You dragged me kicking and screaming into the twenty-first century. Now, Doctor," she added with a coquettish smile, "how about joining my coming out party?"

"I'm afraid I have a previous engagement," Ben said, and managed to appear suitably regretful. "My brother and I have a standing arrangement for him to call every Friday at six."

Geena felt a leap of her heart on Ben's behalf. "Has Eddie been found?"

Frowning, Ben gazed at his shoes. "No, but I like to be home in case he calls."

"Oh. Of course." Her heart plummeted.

"Have you spoken to Tod since last Saturday?" Ben asked her.

Tension brought her shoulders straighter, her head higher. "No. But Carrie has to work all day tomorrow, so I invited Tod to my house."

"She mentioned that when I asked if he could come out with me in the afternoon," Ben said. "If that's okay with you, that is."

"Of course."

"I'll pick him up from your place after lunch."

For all the world as if they were divorced parents with joint custody.

"Okay."

"All right, then."

Their gazes continued to hold. Geena's thoughts flitted between the kiss at the waterfowl refuge and their subsequent argument. If the kiss hadn't been so wonderful, the dispute wouldn't have hurt so much. She wished they could get together and kiss away the conflict, but Ben looked far too unyielding. He wore the authoritative face of medicine rather than that of the caring healing man she was drawn to.

"Geena, if your sister is expecting you, don't feel you have to stay," Greta said, touching Geena on the arm. "Orville will keep me company."

"Be glad to," Orville agreed with alacrity.

"Well, all right, then. I'll drop your parcels off at

your house, Greta. Will they be all right on the porch?"

"Just put them inside the door. It's open."

Geena gave the barber a friendly nudge. "Don't keep her out too late."

Amid blushes from Greta, chuckles from Orville and a terse, "Tomorrow," from Ben, Geena walked to her car. She hated being on the outs with Ben, hated it more than anything—except admitting he was right.

"I LIKE this one." Tod giggled into Geena's mirror with the uninhibited enthusiasm of a child and shook his head from side to side, setting the shoulder-length pink wig swinging.

Tod had been feeling embarrassed about his hair loss as a result of chemotherapy, so she'd brought out her wigs and made a game of trying different styles on Tod. "It's you," Geena agreed. "It goes with your eyes."

That sent Tod into gales of laughter. Geena put her arms around him from behind and hugged him. Physically fragile he might be, but he had a strong spirit.

Ben appeared in the mirror, framed by the doorway behind her. Gran must have let him in and given him permission to climb the stairs to her bedroom.

Geena was suddenly aware of the mess—clothes scattered across the unmade bed, wigs heaped on the vanity table. Well, she'd never claimed to be a neatness fanatic. "Come in."

"Hi, Dr. Ben," Tod said happily. "Look at me."

"Hi, Tod, you wild and crazy guy." Ben moved into the room and picked up a Cleopatra-style wig. "Do you really wear all these?" he asked Geena.

"I used to. I may again. Why not?"

With a sardonic half smile, Ben twirled the wig on his fingers. "Will the real Geena Hanson please stand up."

Geena turned to her reflection in the mirror and saw a slender woman wearing vintage silk and lace, French perfume and no makeup. Was she really such a mystery? "I see her," she said. "Don't you?"

He didn't answer. "I've got a hat you can wear, Tod," Ben said, and produced a bright, multicolored cap with ear flaps and a tassel. "This is what the Guatemalan boys wear in the mountains."

"Cool." Tod pulled off the pink wig and replaced it with the cap. "Can Geena come with us this afternoon?"

"Oh, I can't," Geena said quickly before Ben had to refuse. "Thanks anyway." Geena began to tidy up the wigs. The last thing she wanted was to spend a stilted afternoon with Ben, pretending everything was hunky-dory between them for Tod's benefit. She was sure Ben wouldn't want that, either.

"Of course she can come," Ben said. "Geena?"

"Tod, why don't you run downstairs and ask Gran for a cookie before we go. Ben and I will be right there."

"Okay." Tod ran off without a backward glance.

"You're only asking me along for his sake, aren't you?" Geena demanded.

"Partly. Is that a problem?"

Was it? Maybe it was a problem only if she made it one. "What do you mean by partly?"

The corners of his mouth drooped, and lines deepened around his eyes. "Eddie didn't call again yesterday." His eyes spoke to her more eloquently than words.

He needed her company. The knowledge moved her, but damn it, why couldn't he tell her? She laid a hand on his sleeve. "You should have phoned me last night."

"You weren't home. Besides, what could you have done?"

"I could be a friend," she said simply. "Someone to talk to. Someone who cared."

His jaw tightened, muscles working in an effort to maintain control. Eyes averted, he confessed, "I'm losing hope that he's still alive. It's been weeks. If he was alive, surely he would have contacted some-one by now.''

''There could be many reasons why he hasn't called.''

Ben blinked and pressed the heel of his hand against his eyes. ''He was such a great guy. He wasn't just my little brother—he was my best friend.''

''Don't talk about him in the past tense.'' Geena stepped forward and pulled him into a hug, persisting until his stiff body relaxed and he put his arms around her. His cheek dropped to rest against her temple, and she felt his chest heave in a deep sigh. Comfort flowed both ways; it had been a long time since a man had simply held her. It felt good. ''Don't lose faith, Ben,'' she whispered against his neck. ''He'll come back. I know he will.''

Ben drew away with a lopsided, rueful smile. ''I hope you're right...friend.'' He laid his hand against her cheek, and she felt the warmth right down to her toes. ''Tod and I would enjoy your company today if you'll join us.''

''I'd love to.''

Ben went downstairs to find Tod while Geena quickly tidied up before joining them outside. Then, bundled against the cool October breeze, she strapped herself into the front seat of the Saab. Ben drove out of town along River Road, crossed the highway and continued along the secondary road following the river. She twisted in her seat to glance from Ben to Tod. ''Where are we going?''

Ben's eyebrows rose. ''Didn't Tod tell you?''

Tod spoke from the back seat. ''Sometimes grown-ups change their minds. I didn't want to jinx it by telling.'' His questioning gaze met Ben's in the mirror. Ben nodded.

''So tell me!'' Geena said. ''Now I'm dying to know.''

''Ben's going to get a dog.'' Tod burst out, kicking the back of Ben's seat in his excitement. ''And I get to go over to his house and play with it and pat it and stuff.''

Ben chuckled at Tod's enthusiasm. Geena looked at the profile of his strong jaw, straight nose and high forehead. He was as handsome as he was kind.

''That is so cool!'' she exclaimed. ''I love dogs. Now I'm really glad I came with you guys.''

Ben slowed at a four-way stop to let a farm tractor rumble through the intersection, then consulted a scrap of paper with directions.

''The animal shelter is to the right,'' Geena told him. ''About a mile up.''

Ben made the turn, and within a few minutes they were pulling into the long gravel driveway. Even from a distance they could hear dogs barking, some howling. Ben parked beside the low brick building, and they got out.

Geena smiled at the gleam in Ben's eye. He was every bit as eager as Tod. "I should have guessed you'd be a dog person."

"I always had a dog when I was a kid. But once I was in med school and then interning, I was too busy. Plus, until I went to Guatemala, I lived in the city. It wouldn't have been fair to keep a dog."

Geena paused at the entrance. "Does this mean you don't plan to go back to the city?"

He held the door open for her and Tod. "I guess it does. Hainesville is a thriving community. There's easily work here for two doctors. If Brent Cameron is agreeable."

Interesting.

No one was at the front desk, so they wandered through a set of double doors into the kennels. There, a heavyset man with gray-blond hair straggling around his collar was sweeping the central walkway between the cages, his back to them. Tod ran to the first cage and was greeted with enthusiasm by a big dog with bushy golden fur and a tail that beat time like a metronome.

"Hello," Geena called to the pound attendant, her

eyes widening when he turned. "Dave. I didn't know you worked here."

"Hey, Geena. I clean houses in the morning and work here in the afternoon."

"Are you still volunteering at the fire department?"

Dave leaned on his broom and gazed at Geena with an adoring smile. "Just on the weekends. But I've always got time for a pizza. Just say the word."

"Dave, this is Ben. He's going to buy a dog."

Ben nodded at Dave before wandering over to where Tod was having his fingers licked through the wire mesh. Geena followed. There was something both noble and gentle about the big dog. Her muzzle and face were dark brown, while the long hair that stood away from her head and neck like a lion's mane was richly golden, tipped with auburn. Her pointed ears folded at the tips, giving her a relaxed yet alert expression.

"Her eyes are begging you to take her home," Geena said, dropping to a crouch. "Look! Her tail is talking, too, saying, 'I'll be a good dog.'"

"That's not a dog—it's a bear." Ben held his fingers out for the dog to sniff.

Geena moved on to the next cage. Tumbling over each other in the straw were three roly-poly black pups wagging their stubby tails. "Aren't they gorgeous!"

"Those three are siblings, females from the same litter. We don't get many pups, and when we do, they go quickly." Dave parked his broom beside the wall and came over to the cages. "This one, on the other hand..." He indicated the shaggy golden dog and shook his head.

"Is she going to be euthanized?" Geena asked. Dave nodded. "Oh, Ben, you've got to buy her."

"She's beautiful, Dr. Ben."

"Won't her owners come looking for her?" Ben asked.

Dave shrugged his heavy sloping shoulders. "Haven't so far. She had a collar but no tag. She probably got lost while her owners were on vacation in the area. We can only keep animals thirty days and then we have to put them down."

"I'd prefer to get a younger dog I could train." Ben continued slowly down the aisle between the kennels, stopping to inspect each dog. He reached the end and looked back. The bear made a low whining sound in her throat. Ben could swear she was smiling. He glanced at Dave. "How long has she got?"

Dave glanced at the date on his watch. "She came

in on the fifth of September. Today is the fourth of October. You do the math.''

Tod tugged on Ben's sleeve. ''You can't let her die, Dr. Ben.''

Ben stared at the boy, and Geena could see the debate was all but over. ''No, you're right. I can't.''

''Good man.'' Dave wasted no time in opening the cage. ''You've just bought yourself some instant karma.''

Geena nudged Ben and smiled. ''Even doctors can use a little cosmic assistance now and then.''

Ben took the dog's ruff between his hands and looked her in the eyes. ''I'll call you Ursula.''

Tod's eyes shone, and Geena felt her heart warm to Ben for giving the boy such happiness. Dave let the dog out of the kennel, and man and boy dropped as one to put their arms around the shaggy neck.

Geena turned to Dave. ''How much are the puppies?''

''Fifty dollars each, plus neutering fees and microchip implant for identification.''

''I'll take all three.''

Ben started. ''All three?''

Tod cried out, ''Oh, boy!''

Geena smiled a little sheepishly. ''I know what it's like to be separated from my sisters. I'm not going to let that happen to these girls.''

Dave found a box big enough to hold the three squirming pups and lined it with newspaper. "I'll give you coupons, and when the dogs are old enough, take them to the vet for neutering and the micro-chip."

On the way home, they stopped at the supermarket for dog food and assorted dog paraphernalia—bowls, leads, flea collars. Afterward, they dropped Tod off at home, promising him a chance to visit all four dogs the next day.

"What on earth are you going to do with three dogs?" Ben asked, as he parked outside Gran's house.

Geena smiled. "Oh, I'll think of something."

"It appears to me as if you already have. I'll carry the box in for you."

"Thanks. Oh, good. Kelly's here," Geena said, spying her sister's red station wagon. "I can't wait till she sees her puppy."

Ben's eyebrows lifted. "*Her* puppy?"

Geena gave him a thoroughly mischievous grin. "Don't you dare say a word. She'll take one look, and her mothering instincts will do the rest."

Ben wrestled the box out of the back seat, twisting his head to avoid the trio of cold, moist noses and tongues lapping at him over the edge of the card-board.

"I'll be back shortly," he said through a crack in the window to Ursula, and followed Geena into the house to the big kitchen.

Erin had come over with Kelly, along with all their children, and the appearance of the three puppies among the nine Hanson females caused such an outburst of squealing and carrying on Ben felt like covering his ears.

"Land sakes, child," Ruth wailed to Geena. "What are we going to do with three dogs?"

Geena gave each of her three young nieces a puppy. "I don't think it'll be a problem." She scratched behind the ears of the one Tod had liked best. "This little gal is staying with me, though."

The puppies were squirming so much that the girls sat on the linoleum and let the puppies run around. Ben rescued Erik from his car carrier on the floor before the startled tyke could be clambered all over by the puppies and assaulted by three flapping tongues.

"There's a little too much estrogen flying around the room, wouldn't you say, young fella?" Ben said to Erik as he barricaded himself and the baby behind the kitchen table.

"Thanks, Ben," Erin said, over the heads of Kelly's daughters, before looking down and shrieking. "Oh, no! That puppy just piddled on my Manolo Blahnicks!"

Kelly's eldest daughter, Robyn, pleaded, "Can we have one, Auntie Geena?"

"Oh, yes, please." Beth chimed in, accompanied by much clamoring from the twins, Tammy and Tina.

"It's up to your mom," Geena demurred.

"We've already got a dog," Kelly protested. But she laughed as Robyn poured one of the wriggling puppies into her unresisting arms. The puppy nuzzled her under the chin, and Kelly lapsed into baby talk. "Aren't you just the sweetest little snookums?"

"Getting clucky again, Kel?" Geena flashed a look of pure triumph at Ben.

He rolled his eyes and said teasingly to Erik, "I hope you're paying attention, pal. The softness of women's hearts is exceeded only by the softness of their heads."

Above the general cry of outrage that remark provoked, Geena said, "And who took home the biggest dog in the animal shelter?"

"She only had a day to live," Ben defended himself.

"You're a hero," Miranda proclaimed. She turned to Erin, who was sponging off her shoe at the sink, "Can we take a puppy, too?"

"We live on a houseboat, remember?"

"Dogs can swim. Besides, the McKenzies across the wharf have a dog. And besides that, we're going to move to a house soon so Erik won't crawl off the boat and drown. *Please?*" Miranda pleaded.

Erin sighed. "Ask your father."

"Gran, can I use your phone?"

Ben felt Erik squirm in his arms and glanced down. The baby reached for the drawstring dangling from his jacket hood and tried to tug it toward his mouth. "No, you don't," he said softly, and played with Erik, tugging back and forth on the drawstring. The baby smiled, effortlessly evoking a smile from Ben. It always amazed him how the little devils did that.

He felt someone's gaze upon him and looked up to see Geena watching him. She smiled, glancing from him to the baby. All at once the situation felt a little too domestic.

"I think I hear my dog calling me." He got up and handed Erik to his mother. "Bye, everyone. Enjoy your new puppies."

"Ben," Kelly called as he was leaving. "Max wanted to know if you'd like to join the men's basketball team with him and Nick. It's pretty laid-back, just a bunch of guys deserting their wives for an hour on a Saturday afternoon."

"Sounds good. Tell him to give me a call. The

house is working out great, by the way." He paused. "I suppose I should have found out first if I can keep a pet."

"I know the owner. I'm sure it's okay, but I'll check. Did the plumber come to fix the sink?"

"Yeah, but I'd already got to it myself by then."

"When you're ready to buy," Kelly added with a grin at Geena and Erin, "I specialize in accommodation for future brothers-in-law."

Ben couldn't think of a single thing to say to that so he just nodded and waved goodbye.

Geena walked him to the door and onto the porch. "Don't mind Kelly. She loves embarrassing me."

"What was that about, anyway?"

"Oh, when Nick first came to town she found him the houseboat to rent. Then he and Erin fell in love and got married...." Geena's face turned three shades of pink at the obvious implications of Kelly's line of reasoning. "Of course that has nothing to do with us."

"Of course." He and Geena had problems enough without matchmaking relatives getting into the act.

A howl came from Ursula, who had poked her muzzle out of the window of his Saab. Ben sighed. "I may live to regret that dog."

"I think you did a wonderful thing." She hesitated. "Ben, I was wondering...."

"Yes?" he said, one eye on the car. Ursula had somehow gotten her head through the gap between the window and the frame and was moaning weirdly.

"I've got this...*thing* coming up on the tenth. I was wondering if you'd be my escort."

"*Thing?* What kind of a thing?"

"An evening thing. Dinner, dancing, maybe a cheerleading exhibition..."

Ahrooh. The howl drowned out her last words. A man and woman stopped on the opposite side of the street. The woman pointed at Ben's car.

"Quiet, Ursula. I'm coming," he called to the dog. To Geena, he said, "Not a nightclub, is it?"

"Nothing like that," she assured him. "It's dressy, though."

"I didn't always live in the Guatemalan mountains, you realize. I can rustle up a tux if required."

"A suit and tie will do. So you'll go with me?"

"Where did you say it was?" he asked, over Ursula's wail.

"The town hall. It's my tenth high school reunion." She winced a little as his eyes widened and his jaw dropped.

Ahrooh. "I'd love to."

Her shoulders relaxed, and she let out a breath. "Thanks, Ben. You're the best."

Before he could dash down the steps, she leaned

forward and kissed him. He had an impression of soft lips, spicy sweet perfume and blue eyes. He stepped closer, intending to kiss her properly, when Ursula howled again.

Ahrooh. Reluctantly, he dug his keys out of his pocket and started down the steps. "I'd better go."

At home, he led Ursula to the back porch; he would keep her outside until he found out for sure he was allowed to have a pet.

"Sit," he ordered Ursula, and pointed to the wooden floor. Somewhat to his surprise, she obeyed. He went inside and dug through his trunk for an old woollen blanket. Folded and tucked in a corner of the covered porch, it made a reasonable bed. Ben got her a bowl of water and one of dry food recommended by vets and set them beside the blanket.

She licked his hand, then sniffed the blanket thoroughly. Satisfied, she circled twice and lay down with a deep sigh, as if to say that moving house was tiring and if he didn't mind she was going to rest awhile.

Ben went inside. As he replaced the items he'd removed from the trunk, he came across a box of slides of his Guatemalan village. He slotted them in the handheld viewer and looked over images of his life there. He found his throat closing up more than once at the sight of his friends and patients. The whitewashed adobe houses and colorful native costumes brought back a lot of good times. Then he came to a slide of Eddie, with his shock of blond hair, white-toothed grin and sunburned nose, standing in front of the clinic.

Ben's eyes filled. "Goddamn it, Eddie," he muttered. "Call me, you bastard. I need to know you're okay."

CHAPTER ELEVEN

GEENA HURRIED to answer the doorbell, nervously adjusting the single strap of her off-the-shoulder black silk taffeta dress. In the foyer, she paused long enough to calm her racing heart and check her hair in the mirror, then she opened the door.

"Good evening." Ben's manner was as formal as his perfectly cut evening suit. She could almost hear the click of his heels as he presented her with a white gardenia.

She inhaled its delicious fragrance, noticed her hands were trembling and held it out to him. "Will you do the honors?"

His knuckles brushed her skin as he took the edge of her dress between his fingers, but for once it wasn't being close to him that was giving her the jitters. "A corsage and everything," she said with breathy laughter. "I feel like I'm back in high school."

"Stop fidgeting—I'm afraid I'll poke you with the

pin." His eyes met hers. "Anyone would think you were nervous."

"Nervous? Me?" Geena held her breath, clasped her hands tightly and somehow managed to stand perfectly still until he'd fastened the gardenia to her dress.

"Your turn." She plucked a white rosebud from the overflowing vase on the hall table, cut the stem with scissors from the drawer and tucked it in his buttonhole. "Perfect."

When they arrived at the town hall, the gravel parking lot was already half full, and more cars were arriving. Ben got out and came around to Geena's side while she gathered the shimmering folds of her dress, careful to keep the hem from sweeping the wet ground. It had rained earlier, and water lay everywhere in puddles.

Her anxiety grew as they approached the open front doors of the hall. Geena tightened her grip on Ben's arm. "I'm not so sure this is a good idea."

He studied her as if she were a new and fascinating strain of penicillin. "What exactly are you afraid of?"

If he knew the truth, that she'd never graduated and that at sixteen she'd snatched up a modeling contract at least in part because she'd been afraid of not living up to her sisters' academic reputations, would he still like her? Would he respect her?

She forced a smile and lifted her chin, determined to carry off the charade of self-confidence one more time. "I'm just terrified the guys on the basketball team will remember that I pulled the fire alarm after a game and they had to run out of the showers wrapped in towels."

Ben chuckled and led her into the stream of people flowing through the doors. "Babe, if that's all you've got to worry about, you're laughing."

The hall was decorated with streamers and balloons and a big banner over the stage welcoming everyone to the tenth reunion of the class of '92. In the middle of the floor a disco ball was slowly spinning, reflecting faceted light onto the crowd. Geena scanned the room, searching for familiar faces.

"I see a bar over there," Ben said, speaking above the hubbub. "What can I get you to drink?"

"Mineral water," Geena said automatically, then remembered she was through with depriving herself of all pleasures for the sake of her weight. "On second thought, make that a cosmopolitan, if they have them."

"Living dangerously?" An amused voice came from behind her.

"Linda!" Geena spun and hugged her old friend.

"You look great. How've you been? I called you once and got no answer, then I got busy."

"That's okay." Linda sipped her wine. "With four kids, I know what busy is. Plus, I had the deadline from hell for my latest book."

"Book? I didn't know you were a writer. I mean, I knew about the church newsletter, but that's all."

Linda put her fingers to her lips with a humorous glance at her wineglass. "Oops. *In vino veritas.* I use a pseudonym because I don't want people to know I write novels. I'd appreciate it if you didn't mention it to anyone."

"But why? I think it's wonderful." Linda had always been smart in school, and although Geena hated to admit it, she was still jealous and intimidated by her friend. She could never toss off a Latin phrase as if it were an advertising jingle.

"This is a small town," Linda said. "A lot of people wouldn't understand, especially some of the congregation. Greta Vogler found out because she reads my books, but I swore her to secrecy. I don't *think* she's told anyone." Linda laughed. "What am I saying? If she had, the whole town would know."

"I still don't understand," Geena said, mystified. "What's the big, bad secret?"

Linda glanced around and lowered her voice. "I write *erotica.* It's pretty hot stuff."

Geena's jaw went slack.

"I started when the kids were babies," Linda told her. "If I hadn't found something to occupy my brain in between diaper changes I would have gone bonkers."

"For goodness sake, don't apologize," Geena said. "It's wonderful. You've got to tell me your pseudonym so I can buy your books."

"I'll give you a copy of my latest release when we get together. Hey, there's Heather. You remember her, don't you? She got a Ph.D. in microbiology and does medical research at Washington State University."

"She always was a brain." Geena joined Linda in looking around. "Who else is here?"

"Let's see. Tanya—she's an orthodontist in Simcoe—and Vanessa, who just got a job producing the six o'clock news on channel nine…"

Geena couldn't bear to hear any more. All her former classmates seemed to have gone on to professions that required plenty of brainpower. There must be a few housewives, but raising children was a demanding job, too, as she knew from Kelly, who'd spent the past ten years bringing up four smart and talented girls. All Geena had done for the past decade was look good.

"Toby's around somewhere, probably checking

out the buffet. Hey, there's Larry and Chris," Linda said, waving them over.

"Hi, Larry." Geena greeted the former class nerd, who had morphed into a pretty cool-looking dude with a gorgeous brunette he introduced as Juliet. "Wait, let me guess," she teased the bald-headed man with the paunch who used to be the captain of the football team. "Chris Reardon, right?"

Chris faked a pass with an imaginary football and pulled forward his wife. "Do you remember Loretta? She was in the class behind us."

Ben appeared at Geena's side with her wine. She took a grateful sip before introducing him around and finished by saying, "I think you know Linda Thirsk."

Linda's eyebrows lifted, and she laughed merrily. "Having four children means Dr. Matthews and I are well acquainted. Let's see, so far this summer we've had a broken arm, swimmer's ear, three stitches and..." She frowned, trying to remember.

"Stomach flu." Ben supplied the information helpfully.

"Of course—who could forget the stomach flu!"

"Geena, I've been hearing so many good things about you." Loretta spoke up. "Tod Wakefield is in our son Brandon's class at school. Tod has leukemia," she explained to those who might not know.

"Brandon says Tod's been like a different kid since Geena came on the scene."

Linda touched Geena's arm. "I can't tell you how much I admire you for being able to deal so well with such an emotionally difficult situation. If any of my kids got that sick I just don't think I could handle it."

Geena stared at her. Imagine that, Linda Thirsk admired *her*.

While they'd been talking, Tricia Morrissy, whom Geena remembered had been good at art, joined their group. When she was able to take her gaze off Ben, she chimed in. "My aunt at the aged care facility has been talking about you, too. She said you come to visit regularly."

Geena shrugged. "I get a real kick out of the seniors. They have so many stories, so much wisdom. It's a pleasure to be around them. As for Tod, who wouldn't love such a great kid? He's just so special."

Ben's arm tightened on her waist. "It takes a special person to care."

Linda's gaze moved past Geena's shoulder, and her jaw dropped. "Oh, my God! Is that Miss Vogler?"

Geena had forgotten that most of these people wouldn't have seen Greta's new look yet. Geena had had to coax Greta to try on the sequined evening dress at Briony's, but once she had, Geena could hardly get her out of it long enough to have it wrapped up. She was proud of Greta for wearing it tonight, and gratified that Greta had embraced her new look so completely.

"Good evening," Greta said to their little group.

"Good evening, Miss Vogler," Larry and Chris intoned in spontaneous mimicry of the good old days.

Everyone laughed. Greta glanced around the circle suspiciously, and Geena held her breath, feeling how much of an outsider Greta had always been among the school community. None of the students had liked her, although they'd all feared her sharp tongue and quick frown.

Tonight, a miracle happened. Greta smiled, then laughed, falling in with the joke rather than taking offense as she might have in the old days. She'd even unbent enough to take a drink. She sipped her glass of punch and, in a singsong voice Geena realized with a start was an attempt at friendliness, said, "I'm feeling a bit tipsy. You boys must have spiked the punch."

"If you need reviving, there's a doctor in the house," Ben replied gallantly.

Greta's cheeks flushed pink, and she gave him an arch look. "Now, Dr. Matthews."

"You look great tonight, Miss Vogler," Linda said. "I love your dress. And your hair. I can't get over how different your appearance is."

"Thank you, Linda. I owe it all to Geena. She gave me a makeover for the fashion show. I don't know why I never did it myself. When you think of all the wasted years..." She shook her head.

"Geena's been helping a lot of people," Loretta said. "We were just discussing it."

"*Please.*" Geena wished they'd all shut up about her.

"Geena's a marvel," Greta agreed, then added proudly, "She's working toward her GED and doing very well."

Geena felt her face chill as the blood drained out of it. She was sure everyone in the hall had heard and turned to stare pityingly. Even Ben. She felt his hand slip away from hers as he stepped back to look at her.

"What's a GED?" Larry asked.

"Graduate equivalent diploma," Chris replied. "It's what you go for when you didn't get your high school diploma and are too old to go back to school."

"Oh, yeah," Loretta said. "I forgot Geena left school after grade eleven."

Geena's stomach turned over, and her hands felt

clammy. This was worse than being first down the runway at the opening show of the Paris spring collection. Her nightmare fears had come true—Ben had found out she'd never graduated from high school. He would think she was a complete moron.

"Geena, are you all right?"

She heard Ben's voice as if from a distance, felt his arm reach for her waist and pushed it away. She couldn't face him or her former classmates. Until a few moments ago they'd forgotten she wasn't one of them. Not anymore, thanks to Greta, whose tongue had been loosened by alcohol. Gratitude and pride in a reformed pupil may have motivated her, but why the hell couldn't she keep her mouth shut?

"Excuse me." Geena's voice was a croak. "I...I've got to—"

As she hurried away, she overheard Greta say to Linda in a loud voice, "I *loved* your last book. When's the next one coming out?"

"Book?" Larry said. "What book is that, Linda?"

Geena pushed through the crowd and out the front doors to lean over the railing that ran around the wide steps. The air was chilly after the overheated hall, and goose bumps rose on her bare skin. Small groups of smokers were scattered over the sidewalk in front of the building, punctuating the night air with laughter and clouds of smoke.

"Geena." Ben came up behind her.

She stared ahead, unable to look at him, feeling a complete and utter fraud.

Ben ran his hands up and down her bare arms, warming them with friction. He spoke next to her temple, and his warm breath fanned over her skin. "Why did you run away?"

She took a deep breath and let it out. Chin tilted in the air, cheeks flaming, she replied, "You heard Greta. I never finished high school."

"Geena, Geena, Geena," he murmured. "Beautiful, sophisticated and wealthy, yet you don't have a basic education. Poor little rich girl."

"Don't mock me," she said angrily. "And don't pity me."

"*Pity* you?" He snorted. "Pity is the last thing I feel for you. Why didn't you tell me you were studying for your GED? I'm very interested in this. What are you hoping to do after you earn your diploma?"

"Who knows?" she said flippantly. "Maybe I'll be a brain surgeon."

He turned her around, his hands sliding down her arms to hold her hands. He looked so...hopeful, so pleased. "No, seriously. You wouldn't go to all that trouble unless you planned to use your diploma."

She shrugged and smiled the cool smile she put on to hide her emotions. "Not necessarily. I'm stuck in a small town, recuperating. It's amusing to play school.''

Agitated, she walked away from him, down the steps to the lawn in front of the town hall. He followed.

''Don't you know men admire you and women envy you?'' His arms were around her, warming her. ''Not just because of your beauty, but because you're like…like a sparkler, lighting up the world.''

''A useless butterfly,'' she said bitterly. ''I know that's what you think of me.''

Ben drew back a little and with one finger tilted her chin so he could look at her. ''What with you helping Tod and his family, your visits to the aged care facility and now the GED, I've realized you're not the person I once thought you were.''

''Who *am* I? Even I don't know,'' she cried, breaking free of his embrace. ''I'm changing and I'm scared. I thought I wanted to complete my education to feel good about myself, but the GED doesn't seem relevant anymore. I don't want to learn from books. I just want to be with people and help them in whatever way I can.''

She dropped her arms to her sides, beyond pretense. ''It's so ironic. I wanted you to look past the facade and see the real me. See my hidden strengths. Instead you've uncovered my insecurities.''

Ben took her in his arms again. "Everyone has insecurities. You also have strengths, and they're not hidden. In only a few months you've broken a psychological and physical dependence on cigarettes and pills. You've overcome a potential eating disorder. You've set aside your own problems to help others. Maybe *you're* not seeing the real you."

He kissed her lightly on the mouth. She stood very still, neither pulling away nor softening, instead thinking about what he was saying. Maybe she *had* been too hard on herself.

"Even I have a weakness," he confessed. "You."

She shook her head in denial, but her heart knew a willingness to believe. She was open to love in all its forms; why shouldn't she be open to the love she wanted most?

"I only have to look at you across the room and I forget what I'm doing," he went on. "You smile at me, and I would gladly fling myself across a puddle so you don't get your fancy shoes wet."

Geena smiled and allowed the happiness lurking deep inside to bubble forth. He really meant it. Slowly she slid her arms up his chest to wind them around his neck. "Keep going."

"You're exasperating, infuriating, maddening..." He punctuated his words with tender kisses. "Exciting, enticing, loving..."

His fingertips touched the corners of their joined mouths, then slid down her neck to where blood coursed just beneath the skin, the heat releasing her perfume. The scent mingled with the taste of Ben, the smell of his skin.

Ben. His name filled her mind. She gave herself up to the sensual slide of his hands as they moved down her back, cupping her hips and locking her in tight, as if he couldn't get close enough. Molded to his long, solid body, their hearts beating together, she couldn't escape the feeling, the certain knowledge, that she'd found her other half.

Their previous kisses, each cherished and remembered, like glowing seashells brought out to look at in the dark days of winter, paled in comparison to the white heat of this kiss. Whereas the others had been chaste and tender, mere promises of romance, this was a passionate demand for the ultimate surrender. Frightened and exhilarated at the same time, she knew she wouldn't have to rely on fantasy to get her through tonight. This was the real thing.

He'd seen past the surface to the Geena deep inside. He'd seen her weakness and named it vulnerability. He'd discerned her fragile self-esteem, and his loving words had bolstered her with the knowledge that he cared. He'd seen her weak, flawed, ugly side and wanted her anyway. It made her all the more determined that if she was his weakness, she would also be his strength. She loved him.

Voices, footsteps, people moving past them, returned her to awareness of where they were. She broke the kiss.

"Do you want to go inside?" he murmured, pressing her face to his chest to hide her swollen mouth and love-glazed eyes from the curious gazes of passersby.

Mutely, she shook her head, feeling the rasp of his suit against her cheek and his hard chest beneath her hands. "Let's get out of here."

CHAPTER TWELVE

THEY HURRIED through the parking lot, dodging puddles, breathless with anticipation and urgency. The drive to Ben's house passed with linked hands, intense glances and silence. And then they were out of the car and running up the steps, as if the restraint of the past months was suddenly impossible to keep up another second.

On the front porch, Ben banged his shin on the rough edge of a large cardboard box blocking the doorway. "What the hell..."

"What's that?" Geena asked, but her hands slipped beneath his suit jacket, and she couldn't work up much curiosity about a box.

"Probably Edna got tired of my stuff hanging around her house and had someone bring it over for me."

Ben opened the door and set the box in the foyer, then pulled Geena into his arms. She went willingly, unable to get enough of his mouth or his hands mov-

ing over her body. They started to sink to the car-
peted floor.

Ben dragged them upright. "I want you in my
bed."

All the many times she'd fantasized him making
love to her she'd never imagined that particular
husky quality to his voice. "Take me there."

Reaching his room was a slow process; they stum-
bled along, arms entwined, kissing as they went.
Eventually, she was circling his big bed; peering at
the skylight, through which a shaft of silvery moon-
light fell. She felt free and wild, as though she'd cast
off forever her past, her insecurities and her inhibi-
tions.

"Glorious." She twirled slowly, arms out-
stretched, encompassing the night, the starlight and
the man who already had exceeded her expectations.

Ben tore off his jacket and whirled her in his arms,
sending them laughing and toppling onto the bed. He
knelt, straddling her with his arms and legs, and
dropped a kiss on her lips. She arched upward, torn
between wanting to go slow and savor every moment
and coupling with all the vigor and strength of her
long-pent desire.

When Ben rose on his knees above her to remove
his shirt and she got her first glimpse of his broad,
muscled chest gleaming in the starlight, savoring the

moment lost out to a feverish lust to have him *now*. With a groan, she grabbed his belt and hauled him down on top of her.

For Ben, the feel of Geena's slight body beneath his sparked a wave of hunger to own her. Taking her mouth in a deep kiss, he pressed himself into her, both frustrated and excited by the barrier of their clothes. She moved her hips and stroked his back all the way to his thighs, nearly sending him off the planet.

Breathless, he rolled off her. "You don't know what you do to me. Slow down or it'll be over before we start."

"Then we'll just do it again." She grabbed him by the shoulders and pulled him close enough to kiss. "And again...until we get tired of it."

"I hope you've got stamina...because that won't be any time soon."

He planted kisses down the long diagonal of her off-the-shoulder dress, lingering on the swell of her breast before tugging down the fabric to expose one dark nipple. Her bare breasts were small, but round and full and so beautiful they made him ache. He took her in his mouth and suckled until she moaned with pleasure.

Suddenly, urgently, he was fumbling with his belt, unable to take his eyes off her as she slipped the strap off her other shoulder and stood to let her dress slide off her slender hips. High-cut lace panties and high heels were all she wore. From where he sat her legs seemed to go on forever.

"Ladeez and gentlemen, ze latest look from Goutier," she said, putting on a French accent and a pouty smile. She was watching him watching her, which was extremely erotic. The expression in her eyes told him his desire turned her on.

Slowly, she revolved, presenting him with the slender triangle of her naked back and smooth, rounded buttocks. A tiny heart was tattooed on the high side of one cheek. She struck a pose, hand on jutted hip, gave him a sultry glance over her shoulder, then grinned.

He stood and removed his pants. She swiveled to face him again and, with unabashed longing, ran her gaze over his near-naked body. Her lips parted, showing a glimpse of tongue, as she touched her breast with splayed fingers.

With a raw groan he tossed aside his boxers and pulled her skin to skin in a trembling of chest to breast, throbbing organ to tender belly. Waves of heat rose around them as lips met, tongues tangled, bodies molded. Hands ranged over each other, touching, touching.

Whispers. "Can't…wait…another…second."

Moans. "Need you *now*."

The heat grew until he thought he would spontaneously combust. Reaching behind him, he fumbled at the drawer in the bedside table for the supply of condoms kept in the hope that just this scenario would come to pass. He tried to hand the condom to her.

Smiling, shaking her head, she held up trembling hands. His movements were feverish, but there, it was done, and there was nothing stopping him except...

Eyes locked with hers, he inserted his fingers beneath the waistband of her panties and slid them down. Oh, God, she was shaved clean but for a narrow strip of auburn. Still in her high heels, Geena kicked away the scrap of lace and twined her arms around his neck. He put one hand under her bottom, hoisted her against him and tumbled her onto the bed. She uttered a little shriek, laughed and used their momentum to roll him over until she was on top. He grinned at the unexpected vigor with which she straddled him; how had he ever imagined her fragile?

She leaned forward, her hands on his shoulders and slid herself into position, teasing him and herself with little rocking motions. All he wanted was to plunge in deep, but he gripped her hips and resisted his urges, letting her take control...for now.

"I wanted you from that first day in your office, did you know that?" she said, dipping her head to kiss him lightly on the lips.

"I wanted you, too." He strained upward, taking her nipple in his mouth for a brief hard suck. "But I thought you weren't my kind of woman."

She laughed softly. "And now?"

"Now I know better than to make assumptions where you're concerned." He put pressure on her hips, and she let him slowly pull her down till he filled her completely and she was hot and tight around him. A deep sigh escaped his throat, and he began to move inside her.

He was glad she was on top so he couldn't inadvertently hurt her. He continued to move slowly, half afraid of crushing those small bones with his big hands. But she quickly grew impatient, her breath coming in short gasps, and she rolled off, forcing him on top if he wanted to stay inside her.

"I'm afraid of crushing you," he gasped, trying to moderate his thrusting.

"Don't worry about that. I won't break." Her eyes half-closed in sensual awareness, she gripped him with her legs, with her hands, with her inner muscles. "I like it a little...wild." Her voice was throaty and sexual, and the hard upward thrust of her hips convinced him at last. Assumptions, indeed.

He grinned. "Okay, babe, let's rock and roll."

Unleashed, he drove into her. She met him with a triumphant cry. Their bodies collided, rolled and collided again, intensifying the pleasure. She was stronger than he'd thought, supple and athletic in a way that got him very excited. His skin became slick with sweat; she glowed with the flush of arousal. He couldn't break eye contact with her burning gaze even long enough to kiss her. She laughed, exultant, and he rolled her again, right off the bed, to land with a thud on the blanket-strewn floor.

"You okay?" He gasped, and she nodded. Holding her to him, he picked her up and fell on the bed. With a laughing, whooping cry, she strained against him, pulling him farther into her. They moved with increased intensity. One heart, one mind, one final burst of energy, exploding into fire as they labored to become...one...flesh.

An eerie, breathy cry escaped Geena as she climaxed. The last note still hung in the thick musky air when he arched his rigid body above her and responded with a groan from the depths of his soul.

For uncounted moments he sank into oblivion. When he came to, he and Geena were still clinging, arms and legs wrapped around each other. They were facing the wrong end of the bed, the blankets were on the floor and the bottom sheet was ripped half off.

He touched her swollen mouth and asked once more, "Are you okay?"

Dazed, her eyes blinked open, and she gave him a smile that laser beamed its way to his heart. "I'll never be the same again, but to answer your question, yeah. Fantastic."

"That was sure something."

She grinned. "Something good?"

"You know it was." He drank her in—her slightly smudged eyes, porcelain skin and full lips. There was a word for what he felt, maybe lots of words: *wonder, satiation, contentment, connection...*

Love.

Acknowledging the truth of his emotions was a relief and a blessing. Nothing had ever felt so right. And yet...

He touched her cheek with his fingertips, wanting to tell her he loved her, yet afraid it was too soon to be sure of his feelings. Afraid he was so adrift from logic that he couldn't tell love from infatuation.

Gradually, muscles locked in place wanted to stretch. Slowly, carefully, they untangled their limbs, and he eased himself out of her.

He glanced down and swore.

"What is it?" she asked languidly.

"We were *too* wild. The condom tore." His worried gaze met hers.

Geena laughed a little sadly. "I haven't had a period for over a year, remember? I can't get pregnant."

"Plenty of breastfeeding mothers have thought the same thing, to their subsequent chagrin."

Her slender shoulders rose in a graceful shrug. "We can't do anything about it now." Then she traced the outline of his mouth with the tip of her finger. "Next time I'll go easier on you."

His insides warmed at her chuckle, and he planted a dozen or so kisses around her face, ending behind her ear, making her giggle. Reluctantly, he eased off the bed. "Let me go get rid of this."

Geena sank into the pillows, bathed in starlight. Her body felt heavy with a satisfied ache, but her heart had never felt so buoyant, so laugh-out-loud, thistledown light. A light came on in the bathroom, and she heard water running. She almost wished they *had* just started a baby. With the thought, a dialog began in her head.

Mom promised.

Ben wouldn't want the complication.

He'll make a fantastic father.

They had unresolved issues.

A baby, what joy!

Ben returned with a warm, damp cloth and gently wiped the stickiness and the sweat from her body.

He was so thoughtful, so strong and tender. Cool air tingled across her skin in the wake of the cloth. His eyes followed the movement of his hand against her flesh, turning the heat up again.

She drew him into her arms, and he tossed the cloth aside to cover her body with his. Their love-making this time was slow and intense, a languorous rhythm of minimum motion and maximum sensation. Geena savored the warm velvet of his skin, the musk scenting the air around them, the slip and slide and pulse of two bodies moving intimately, slowly rocking toward a simultaneous shuddering, quivering release.

Afterward, she lay in his arms, gazing into his dark eyes, still bound like one enchanted by the deep emotional connection they'd just experienced. If Milan had taught her anything it was that life was too short and relationships too important not to say what she felt.

"I love you," she whispered.

He opened his mouth, and quickly she placed a finger against his lips before he could speak. She'd seen the flash of wariness in his eyes. It didn't matter. "I know it's too soon to say that, but my heart is shouting it out." He tried again to speak, and she stopped him with a kiss. "Your actions are telling me everything I need to know right now. Promise you won't say you love me until your heart is shouting it out to you?''

He nodded, and she took her finger away.

"I *think* I'm—'' he began.

"Shh. Don't think.'' She snuggled against him, content. It didn't matter that his heart hadn't yet caught up to his body; she and Ben belonged together. Someday he'd know that, too. For now, she was utterly blissful simply feeling his long fingers in her hair and his warm breath on her forehead.

Ben broke the silence. "I can't believe Greta told all your old friends you're studying for the GED.''

Geena moaned. "I don't want to talk about Greta.''

"I won't say another word.'' He massaged her scalp with his fingertips, sending her into purring mode.

But once Greta had been introduced, she stuck in Geena's mind. "I wonder why she never married. They say she was jilted when she was young, but it seems odd she never found anyone else.''

An odd quality to Ben's silence made her push away from him. "You know something. Tell me!''

He shook his head. "Patient confidentiality.''

"Oh, you're no fun.''

"That's not what all the girls tell me.'' A teasing light appeared in Ben's eyes. His fingers moved to her breast, tracing a tingly path around her nipple. "As your doctor, I'm happy to inform you I've got a cure for that insatiable itch of yours."

He lowered his mouth to begin a gentle sucking. Her blood started to heat, and she lost all interest in figuring out what made Greta tick. He drew back briefly to regard her peaked nipple with satisfaction while his hand worked its way down her belly to the juncture of her thighs.

"That itch is getting worse, Doctor," she murmured, and wrapped her hand around his pulsing member.

"I'll just insert a little something to ease the ache." Ben gently pushed her legs apart.

She gazed at him wide-eyed, titillated by the game they were playing. "Ooh, that's a *big* something."

"That means it's time for the next stage of treatment." He moved inside her. "Now, how does that feel?"

"Mmm, very nice..."

SOMETIME, perhaps hours later, Geena awoke in darkness. The stars were obscured by clouds, and rain drummed the windows and skylight. Sleepily, she stretched out an arm, seeking Ben's warmth. He was gone.

Blinking, she pushed herself up on her elbows and

noticed a thin line of yellow light coming from beneath the shut door. The digital clock beside the bed told her it was 6:14. Ben was an early riser; in the summer she'd often seen him jogging before going to the clinic. But this was October, and it was still dark out. Besides that, they hadn't gotten much sleep.

She got out of bed, found Ben's shirt on the floor and put it on. Scraping her hands through her hair, she went to the living room. Ben was sitting on the sofa in his boxers, his large frame oddly still. The cardboard box he'd found on the porch stood open before him, and a piece of paper dangled from one limp hand. She was about to tease him about loving and leaving her when he glanced up. Her words died in her throat at the sight of his grief-stricken face.

"Ben! What is it?" She dropped to the sofa at his side, her arms instinctively circling him. "Ben, are you all right?"

He swallowed as if he had a golf ball in his throat, then slowly turned his head. His eyes, so full of love and laughter just hours before, were lifeless.

"Ben, you're scaring me. What is it?"

"Eddie." He gestured helplessly to the box. Tears welled, and he shook his head, unable to speak.

Letting go of him, Geena pulled the box toward her. A torn and muddy backpack lay atop a jumble of clothes. Below that were some books, a toiletry bag with a safety razor, a tattered copy of the photo Ben had on his desk and one of an older couple—Ben and Eddie's parents, Geena assumed. Below that was a sweatshirt emblazoned Texas University. Wrapped inside the sweatshirt was a Mayan clay figurine of a pregnant woman, which had miraculously survived the disasters.

Ben picked up the figurine and squeezed his eyes closed, covering his face with a shaking hand. "Eddie bought this at the market the day he walked me to the bus that would take me to Guatemala City. Some of this stuff they salvaged from the ruins of the clinic. Some of it they found on the mountain."

"What does this mean?" she whispered, afraid.

Ben handed her the paper, wet with his tears. She glanced at the letterhead—International Médicos—then scanned the brief typewritten message, dazedly trying to take it in.

Edward Matthew's effects... All that could be salvaged from the flood and earthquake-damaged clinic... Dr. Matthews was last seen on the path up Volcán Santa Maria, the site of the worst mud slides. His backpack was found many miles downstream, but his body has not been recovered. After extensive searching we regret to inform you that Dr. Matthews is presumed dead.

A sob tore from her throat, and she reached for Ben, pulling him into her embrace. "Oh, Ben. I'm so sorry."

She felt his shoulders shake with the effort of holding in his pain; then, with a strangled moan, he let himself go and cried in her arms, clutching her, wetting her neck with his tears. She rocked him as she would a child, murmuring comforting phrases in the hope she could wipe out the starkness of death.

At last he lay with his head in her lap, his body curled on the sofa. "It's my fault," he muttered. "All my fault that Eddie's gone."

"How can you say that? He's—he was a grown man, responsible for his own actions. He chose to go to Guatemala. You didn't force him."

"He looked up to me and tried to do what I did...ever since he was a kid. He was too young to be careful of his own safety. He still thought he was immortal."

Geena stroked Ben's hair from his temple, finger combing the dark strands into smooth waves. "He *is* immortal. He's gone to—"

Ben's hand tightened on her bare knee. "Don't."

"The light," she finished. "Ben, whether you believe or not, I know Eddie's in a good place. He's found peace and joy."

Ben sat up abruptly, scowling as he dragged a hand through his hair, erasing the effects of her touch. "He's *dead*. Dead before his time."

"Listen to me. Just listen." She put a hand on his shoulder when he would have jumped to his feet. "Please."

With bad grace he threw himself on the couch. "What is it?"

Geena took a deep breath and reminded herself he was so brusque only because he was hurting. If he knew what awaited Eddie, his pain would be less. She loved Ben, and so she told him every detail of emotion and sensation associated with her near-death experience. *Every* detail, not omitting the part where her mother told her she was going to have a baby.

Ben listened impatiently, now and then uttering a snort of disbelief. When she was finished, he kicked the box aside and got to his feet. "For God's sake, Geena," he said violently, "my only brother is dead and in my darkest hour of grief you try to comfort me with fairy tales!"

"Ben—"

"I gave you those medical articles refuting near-death claims. Didn't you read them?"

"Yes, but—"

"So how can you sit there and tell me you still believe in that crap?"

Geena regarded him with wooden detachment. She'd thought they had connected on some deep, unassailable level. She'd bared her soul to him; he'd shown her his most tender side. Yet still he rejected her experience. He rejected *her*. She'd been mistaken about him. Their relationship was just as superficial as any in her past.

For the love she bore him, she tried again. "Isn't science based on empirical evidence?" She'd learned that studying for her GED. He nodded. "Well, I have empirical evidence to support what I say. I *experienced* firsthand what Eddie has now experienced, and I know he's not suffering."

"Eddie's dead!"

"Ben, you're in shock. That will pass, and when it does, I hope you'll find comfort in what I've told you."

"What about the people who are revived after clinical death who don't experience anything, just blackness?"

She spread her hands. "I admit, I can't explain that."

"Aha!"

"But it doesn't negate my experience." She threw a cushion aside and got to her feet. "Can't you even try to open your mind? Can't you accept for one moment that there are more things in heaven and on earth than are dreamed of in your philosophy?'' she asked, paraphrasing Shakespeare.

She smiled bitterly. Her GED studies were coming in handy.

''It's easy for you to talk—you're *alive*.'' He shot the words back. ''If the afterlife was so blissful, why didn't you stay dead?''

''I explained to you about that,'' she said, wounded by his callous sarcasm. ''I had to come back, for my child.'' He wasn't the perceptive, enlightened man she thought he was if he couldn't see past his scientific prejudices and accept that she just might be telling the truth.

''Oh, yeah, the child. You're not even consistent. You can't get pregnant, remember? You're too thin. I don't know what I was thinking, falling for someone as flaky as you.''

Her heart shriveled at his cutting tone and cruel words. ''My near-death experience was the most profound occurrence of my life. If you can't understand and accept that, then there's no hope for us.''

She waited for him to say something to bridge the gulf that had risen so abruptly and so unexpectedly between them. He stared at her, locked in pain, unable to see beyond his grief.

"I'll get dressed," she said quietly. "Then I'd like you to drive me home."

Twenty minutes later, she let herself into Gran's quiet, dark house and crept up the stairs. Only after she showered and crawled into bed did she let her tears flow. Time would eventually heal Ben's sorrow, but eternity wouldn't be long enough to reconcile their differences.

CHAPTER THIRTEEN

BEN DIDN'T SLEEP after taking Geena home. He prowled the house, alternately numb with grief and cursing God for the injustice of his little brother's death. At last he called his parents. Telling his mother that her son was gone was the hardest thing he'd ever had to do. Ben listened to her weep on the phone and felt as though he'd let everyone down by not taking care of his little brother. Ursula whined and pushed her muzzle into his palm.

"That's all the letter from International Médicos said," he told her when his mother calmed down enough to ask for details. "No, I doubt it would do any good to go down there and search for him. The last time I talked to the regional coordinator she said that section of the western highlands is still ravaged by the floods. I'll fly to Austin next Saturday.

"I can't get there sooner," he said when she begged him to come right away. "I have a little boy about to start his next round of chemo. I need to be

here in case he or his mother need me. Yes, I'll remember to bring Eddie's things. I love you.''

He hung up the phone and sank to the floor, and
Ursula put a paw on his shoulder and tried to lick
his face. ''It's okay, girl. Everything's going to be
okay.'' But it wasn't, and it never would be again.
Where Eddie had been, there was now a hole in the
universe.

On Monday, Ben struggled to give his patients the
attention they deserved. Underlying his anguish over
his brother's death was the knowledge that his relationship with Geena was beyond repair. He knew
she'd only tried to make him feel better and that he
shouldn't have taken his grief out on her, but boy,
was she misguided.

Her comment about him not having an open mind
had stung. He'd always prided himself on being re-
ceptive to new ideas, new ways of doing things. But
near-death experiences? They were right out there
with New Age crystals and laetrile, as far as he was
concerned. A conversation with her deceased
mother? She might as well ask him to believe in
ghosts. And in a dentist's waiting room? He shook
his head. It all sounded too much like something
Geena would make up. As for her thinking he might
derive comfort over Eddie from that concoction, it
beggared belief.

After his last patient had left, he called the hospital to see how Tod's treatment had gone.

"I'm sorry, Dr. Matthews, there's no record of Tod Wakefield being admitted here today," the nurse in the oncology unit told him.

Ben drew a hand over his face. He hadn't slept last night, and his nerves were ragged. But he'd talked to the pediatric oncologist on Friday and he knew for a fact Tod was scheduled for today. "Check your records again, please."

"I already double-checked, sir. Would you like to speak with the ward nurse?"

"Put her on."

A minute later, a brisk voice said, "Molly Ranelagh here. Yes, Dr. Matthews?"

"I'm calling about a young patient of mine, Tod Wakefield. He was supposed to undergo chemo today, but I understand he hasn't been admitted."

"Mrs. Wakefield phoned this morning to cancel treatment." Nurse Ranelagh's voice sharpened. "I presumed the decision was made in consultation with Tod's doctor."

A vein started to throb in Ben's temple. "Was she postponing this treatment session for some reason?"

"Oh, no, she was removing him from the program. She was very definite about that. She sounded...I don't know...*happy*. We're short-staffed at present, and I haven't had a chance to review Tod's file. I assumed he must have gone into remission.''

"He's not in remission," Ben said heavily, consulting Tod's file. "His last white blood cell count taken two weeks ago was higher than it's ever been.''

He said goodbye to Nurse Ranelagh and grabbed his coat. All the way to Tod's house, Ben fought a sinking feeling. Terminal cancer patients sometimes opted to discontinue treatment, but they were usually elderly, with no hope. Tod was by no means terminal; he had an excellent chance of recovering—if he was treated.

Carrie opened the door wearing a long tie-dye dress and shards of amethyst crystals set in silver around her neck. The trill of birdsong and the sound of a waterfall startled Ben until he heard an accompanying harp and realized the music was coming from the stereo in the living room. A sweetish herbal scent tickled his nostrils.

"Hi, Dr. Matthews. Are you here to see Tod?" Carrie stepped back to allow him entry.

"I'm here to talk to you, Carrie. Do you have a moment?''

"Sure. Billy is napping, and Tod is in his room.'' She led the way into the living room. An ankle bracelet strung with tiny bells jingled when she walked. "Can I get you some herbal tea?''

"No, thank you." He sat on the edge of a worn couch and unzipped his jacket. "I've just been talking to the hospital. I was surprised to discover Tod hadn't gone in for his treatment."

Carrie sank onto a rocking chair and flipped her long hair out of her eyes. Reaching into a cloth bag on the floor beside her, she pulled out a crochet hook and several balls of vividly colored yarn. "I loved the woven Guatemalan hat you gave him. I've been trying to copy it."

"I'm glad you liked it. About Tod's treatment…"

With the crochet hook in her right hand, she twisted red yarn around her fingers in an intricate pattern and positioned the circle of crocheting where she'd left off. "I probably should have told you sooner, but I knew you weren't going to like it."

She was right. The harp was beginning to get on his nerves, too. "Told me what?"

The crochet hook wound in and out. Carrie's smile was serene. "I canceled Tod's next round of chemotherapy."

"I know that." He rubbed his fisted knuckles. "What I don't understand is *why*. Is it the cost? We can arrange some kind of loan or plan a fund-raiser." Hell, he'd *give* her the money if he thought she'd accept it.

Carrie shook her head. "It's not the money."

"I know Tod gets very sick with the chemo, but believe me, it's better than the alternative." He let that hang; they both knew the alternative was death.

"That's just it. You see…" She paused in her crocheting to search for words. "Tod's going to be okay. He doesn't need any more treatment."

Too stunned to speak, Ben stared at her. Where the hell had Carrie gotten the idea Tod didn't need treatment? A cold prickling scurried over his skin. *Geena.* He'd been afraid of fallout from her offhand remark to Tod at the waterfowl refuge, but he'd never imagined Carrie Wakefield would go this far.

"Tod's latest white blood cell count was very high," he reminded Carrie. "He's not in remission by any stretch of the imagination. Let's not mince words here—Tod needs treatment or he could die."

"Geena told Tod it wasn't his time," Carrie countered with absolute certainty. She leaned forward, elbows on her knees. "Geena died and came back to life, Dr. Matthews. She's the nearest thing to an angel we'll ever hope to see. If she says it's not Tod's time to die, I believe her. She's been to Heaven and back. *She knows.*"

Oh, God. This couldn't be happening. Ben wanted to push his hands into his hair and tear it out by the roots. He wanted to shake Carrie. He wanted to strangle Geena. He made himself stay calm and steepled his hands in front of him. "Geena isn't a doctor. She can't make that prognosis."

"I would do anything for my son," Carrie went on as if Ben hadn't spoken. She was gently rocking. "But I won't put Tod through another round of chemotherapy if he doesn't need it. Maybe if he's not sick so much he'll get better."

Ben blinked in disbelief at her insane logic. Ignorance was no excuse. Both he and the pediatric oncologist had explained in detail the illness and treatment.

He rubbed both hands over his face, suddenly feeling every wakeful minute of the past two nights. Planting both fists on his thighs, he exhaled a deep sigh. "Carrie, whatever Geena experienced, it didn't give her omniscient powers. She doesn't know Tod's fate, any more than I do. With the help of modern medicine and a positive attitude, I believe Tod can overcome his illness, but I wouldn't dare leave it to faith alone."

Moisture shone in Carrie's eyes, and her rocker moved faster in the first sign of agitation she'd displayed so far. "Some days faith is all that keeps me going, Dr. Matthews. Geena's given me new hope."

"Nevertheless, I want you to reconsider. This is a life-and-death decision. With proper treatment, leukemia patients have a better than seventy-five percent chance of survival. Those are pretty good odds, but the key is treatment."

She pulled on the yarn. "Western medicine doesn't have all the answers, Dr. Matthews."

"It's the best system we've got."

"Oh, don't worry. I'm not leaving Tod's fate completely in the lap of the gods," Carrie said, smiling.

Thank goodness for that.

"I've started Tod on herbal therapy."

For crying out loud, he expected this kind of thing in remote mountain villages of Guatemala, not in modern America. "Did Geena recommend that?"

"She doesn't even know about it yet." Carrie glanced at her watch and put her crocheting away. "I've got to get ready for work, so if you'll excuse me…"

Ben rose. "I can't just drop this matter, Carrie. I'm going to ask the oncology pediatrician to talk to you. Will you listen?"

She shrugged. "Sure, I'll listen, but he'll be wasting his time."

Outside the door, Ben paused. "What does Tod think about canceling his treatment?"

"He's just happy he won't get sick or lose any more hair. He believes in Geena, too."

Ben left Carrie and drove directly to Geena's house. He strode up the walk, his fists clenching and unclenching as he tried to contain his anger. Ruth Hanson opened the door to his pounding and, looking somewhat apprehensive at his air of restrained violence, told him Geena was at the town hall, helping the ladies practice for the fashion show on Saturday.

In the hall, techno music blasted from a boom box. Geena stood before the stage, exhorting Mabel Gribble as she sashayed her considerable bulk down a makeshift ramp. "Remember the SHH principle, Mabel—shoulders over hips over heels."

Mabel got to the end of the ramp, saw Ben stride in, scowling, and froze.

"You're not supposed to get stage fright in front of an empty room, sweetie," Geena called, her back to Ben. "Now, jut your right hip, pivot and glide home."

Mabel pointed behind Geena. Geena turned.

"Ben." She came forward, smoothing her hair. "I didn't hear you come in. What do you think? The music will be better on the night, of course...." Her voice died away as she saw the expression on his face. "What's wrong?"

Ben noticed the huddle of women in evening dress onstage, watching. "Is there a room somewhere we can be alone?"

"Sure." She glanced around, then led him to a

door in the far wall that opened into a kitchen. "Would you like coffee?"

"This isn't a social call—" he grated the words out "—and my feathers will not be unruffled by a dose of caffeine. We need to talk."

She glanced at him uncertainly. "Okay, but can you make it quick? The ladies can't seem to make a move without me."

"This is important. It's about Tod."

Fear leaped into her eyes. "What happened?"

"Nothing...*yet,*" he said. "But thanks to your careless remark to Tod about it not being his time, Carrie has canceled Tod's chemotherapy."

Geena's hand flew to her mouth. "Oh, my God." She hesitated. "I suppose the treatment is necessary?"

How could she even ask that question? "Only if we want Tod to recover," he said grimly.

Her ivory skin paled to a sickly hue. "But why would Carrie take my word over a doctor's that Tod doesn't need further treatment?"

"She thinks you're an angel with divine knowledge. You think you can crook your little finger and get your own way. Well, I've got news for you, sweetheart. This is cancer. You don't just say, 'No, I don't want that for my little friend,' and the disease goes away."

"Wait just a minute!" She glared at him, eyes blazing. "You make me sound as though I'm crazy or something. Telling Tod and his mom about my near-death experience helped them cope with the possibility of death. Far better than that stupid book you sent over."

"I'll concede the book may not be as good as some, but *you* taught them not to be afraid. You got them thinking death is okay. Speaking as a doctor, and as a caring human being, I say death is *never* an acceptable outcome for a nine-year-old boy with his whole life ahead of him."

"But…" She floundered.

"And in case you've forgotten, you're not *qualified* to counsel cancer patients."

She winced but countered quickly, "I have something better than book learning. I've *been* there. *And back.*"

Ben paced the room, sweeping a hand out. "If you want to believe in fairy tales, fine. But don't go telling them to an impressionable young boy and his desperate mother. Surely you could see how susceptible Carrie is to alternative ideas. Knowing that, how could you have said what you did?"

"Carrie's not crazy, either. She just has a different way of looking at things." Geena pointed a finger at him. "You're still angry over Eddie."

"Forget Eddie for the moment. I'm here about Tod. As you said, he's a special little boy." Emotion choked Ben, and he had to stop and take a deep breath. "I don't want to lose him. And I'm not just speaking as a doctor."

"I know." Geena's eyes glistened. "Oh, Ben, I feel the same way. I'll talk to Carrie. I'll make her understand."

For a moment Ben wanted to reach out and pull her into a hug that would comfort them both. The thought of Tod made his anger resurface. If Geena had lowered the boy's chance of survival by even one percentage point, he wasn't sure he could ever forgive her.

"Don't bother," he said. "She's gone to work. And anyway, you've done enough damage."

A timid face peered around the door. "Excuse me, Geena. Miranda wants to know if she's allowed to wear four-inch heels. Erin thinks she's too young."

Geena sighed and rolled her eyes. "I'll be there in a minute, Marie. I'm still talking to Dr. Matthews."

Ben walked out with a dismissive wave of his hand. "Forget it. We're done."

"I'll fix it, Ben," she called after him. "I won't let Tod down. I promise."

He turned so she could see the warning in his eyes. "Stay away from Tod and his mother."

BUT GEENA was determined *not* to stay away. If she had caused a problem, she had to fix it. Ben was right that she should have thought before speaking, but she'd never imagined Carrie would interpret her words as gospel.

Several days passed before she could catch up with Carrie. During that period, she traveled to Everett and sat the exam for the graduate equivalent diploma. Although she'd studied hard for several months and Greta assured her she would do fine, Geena found it hard to get excited about the test or care about the results. She put in the best effort she was capable of at the time, but all she could think about was Tod. Would Carrie reverse her decision? Was Tod going to make it?

Thursday found her and Merri standing on the Wakefields' front porch. Geena remembered to knock because the doorbell was broken.

"Hi!" Carrie welcomed her warmly, making Geena feel even more guilty, then glanced at the black puppy twining itself around Geena's ankles. "If you're looking for Tod, he's at school."

"I really came to see you." She'd only brought the dog for Tod to play with in case he was at home. This wasn't a conversation she wanted him to hear. "Are you sure I'm not disturbing you?"

"No. I'm always glad to see you. I was just about to make a pot of green tea. Want some?"

"That would be great."

Carrie led the way to a tiny kitchen painted in orange and blue. The cork floor was strewn with toys, and the fridge was decorated with Tod's artwork. Billy sat in his high chair and banged his arms on the tray when he saw Geena.

Merri started to chew on a plastic ride-on toy, and Geena dragged her away before she could do damage with her sharp little teeth. She hoisted the dog onto her lap and bent to whisper in a furry black ear. "These pants are Yves St. Laurent originals, sweetie. Remember your house training."

Carrie set floral teacups and mismatched saucers on the table. "I found these funky old bone china cups in the secondhand shop in Simcoe. I swear they make the tea taste better."

"Gran has a collection of good china teacups, but she never uses them because they don't go in the dishwasher."

Carrie smiled as she filled the kettle. "I don't have to worry about that. *I'm* the dishwasher. By the way, I'm giving a class in meditation at the rec center next month if you're interested."

"I might be," Geena murmured. The more she and Carrie had in common, the harder it became to say her piece. In need of fortification, she spooned two scoops of sugar into her cup. Merri sniffed the edge of the table, eager for whatever scraps she might find. "Down, girl."

"Tod and I had a wonderful day the other week." Carrie spooned leaf tea into a big brown teapot. "I'm so grateful to you for taking Billy again for a few hours."

"I was glad I could help." Geena decided the time had come to get to the point. "Dr. Matthews told me you'd canceled Tod's chemotherapy treatment."

Carrie beamed. "Thanks to you."

"Please," Geena said, holding up a hand. "I don't want to be responsible for this." At Carrie's hurt look, she went on, "When I told Tod it wasn't his time, I never meant that he didn't need further treatment. You should trust Dr. Matthews and the oncology pediatrician. They know Tod's medical needs better than I."

"But you've seen the supreme being. You know things the doctors can't know."

Supreme being, the light, God—all names for the same entity as far as Geena was concerned. "In my heart, I believe I *did* see God, but that doesn't give me the ability to predict the future. While I hope with all my soul that Tod will recover, I can't possibly know for sure he will."

Carrie frowned in silence as she poured boiling water into the teapot. "Then why did you say it wasn't Tod's time?"

"Because I want so much for him to get well. The possibility that he might not seems inconceivable. My words were irresponsible. I never dreamed you and Tod would take them literally."

To her horror, Carrie began to cry, her tears sliding unchecked down her cheeks. "It's not your fault. I wanted to believe so much that you were right. I've tried everything—crystals, pyramids, herbs, meditation... Tod is just a baby, my first baby. If I lose him... Oh, Geena, I'm so afraid." She dropped into a chair, laid her head on her arms and sobbed. Billy, seeing her, began to sniffle, then cry.

Geena pushed Merri to the floor, ignored Billy for the moment and put her arms around Carrie. "Don't be afraid. Never be afraid. That's one thing I *do* know," she said, stroking Carrie's long hair. "I believe with all my heart there *is* an afterlife. I believe that God is love, and love is all that matters."

Carrie raised her tear-streaked face. "Yes, yes, I believe that, too. But I can't stop feeling bad. You have no idea. I lie awake at night for hours, dreading what the future might hold. I can't stand seeing Tod suffer." She reached for her crying baby, rocking him to try to soothe him. The two of them cried together.

"I don't want to make light of your fears and grief. I have no right to," Geena said, her arm around Carrie's shoulder. "You're going through a horribly difficult period. I just want you to know—I'm here for you and Tod and Billy. Whatever I can do. Anytime."

"Thank you," Carrie said, wiping her eyes with her sleeve. "I'm sorry. I don't usually break down like this. I have to be strong for my kids."

"And you are. You're doing a marvelous job."

They heard the front door bang and Tod's voice in the hallway. "Mom, I'm home. What's there to eat?"

Carrie handed Billy to Geena and went to the sink to dash cold water on her face. She drew a deep breath and let it out, composing her face in a manner that spoke of plenty of practice. She smiled wanly at Geena. "I can't believe there was ever an instance when I got impatient hearing him say he was always hungry." Her smile faded. "Chemo will bring back his nausea."

Geena squeezed her hand. "It's only temporary. If treatment cures him, the discomfort is worth it, right?"

Carrie sighed deeply. "Yes, but—"

"So you'll talk to Ben about putting Tod back on chemotherapy?"

"I'll think about what you've said."

Tod had been standing, unnoticed, in the doorway. He ran to his mother's side. "Do I have to, Mom? Geena said it wasn't my time."

Carrie slid an arm around her son and pulled him to her side. "It isn't. We've got to believe that. Whatever happens, we're going to love each other just as hard as we can."

Geena stood and touched Tod on the shoulder. "Take care, Mr. Buster. I probably won't see you for a while."

Tod lifted his uncomplicated gaze to hers. "Why not?"

Because Ben had told her not to. Because she'd lost confidence in herself. Because she couldn't bear to risk hurting Tod in any way. Because with nothing left between her and Ben, she couldn't stay in Hainesville. All of the preceding. And none of which she could say to this child.

Holding back her tears, she put on a smile and tugged on the straps of the multicolored cap Ben had given him. "I might be going back to work as a model after the fashion show." She added to Carrie, "My agent has been after me to accept a job in Paris."

Tod cried, "But I let the beetle go, and I need you to help me find a new one."

"Next time." She tweaked his nose, pretending to pinch it off between her fingers. "Oops, look at that. I got your nose."

Tod tried halfheartedly to snatch her thumb.

Geena noticed a paperback sticking out of his jacket pocket. "What are you reading?" Tod showed her the cover. *"Nose Pickers from Outer Space,"* she read. "Gross."

Tod giggled and made spooky fingers coming for her. And just when she thought she would get out of there without crying, his smile faded and a worried look came into his eyes. "Are you really going away?"

Geena bit her lip. "Oh, Tod. I'll be thinking of you every minute. I'll send you a special present for Christmas, okay? Can you smile for me?" Tod gave her a watery smile, and she hugged him close so he couldn't see the tears filling her eyes. "That's my Mr. Buster."

CHAPTER FOURTEEN

FRIDAY NIGHT, Geena was organizing her outfits for the fashion show when the doorbell rang. She hurried down the hall, hoping Mabel Gribble wasn't having another crisis with the flowers or the music. She swung open the door and stepped back, startled. "Ben. What are you doing here?"

Ursula surged against the lead in his hand, and Geena dropped to her knees to pet the big dog, glad of an excuse to avoid Ben's eyes. Her heart was beating like crazy; despite everything, she still loved him.

"I'm going to Austin. My parents have arranged a memorial service for Eddie. I'll stay with them for a few days afterward."

"Do you want me to take care of Ursula?"

"No, I'm taking her over to the Wakefields'. I just came to say goodbye."

Oh, please, not goodbye. He didn't know how final that was. She would be gone by the time he got back.

She rose and went to the drawer in the hall table where she'd left a check she'd written. "I was going to mail this to you,'' she said, handing it to him. ''It's a contribution to the relief effort in Guatemala.''

Ben glanced at the check, and a muscle in his jaw twitched. ''Ten thousand dollars?''

''If you want more, I can add a zero.''

''This is fine. It's more than fine. It's extraordinarily generous. You're already doing the fashion show to raise funds.''

''I wanted to make a personal contribution.'' She'd recently pledged a similar amount to cancer research.

''As I said, it's very generous. Thank you.'' He started to go.

''Ben!''

''What?''

''How's Tod? I've been so worried.''

''Carrie's going ahead with Tod's treatment.''

Geena sagged with relief. ''Thank God she changed her mind!''

''The chemo has been delayed because the hospital canceled Tod's time slot, but he's been rescheduled.''

Geena twisted her fingers together. ''He won't... the delay won't...I mean, one week isn't going to make a difference, is it?''

He made her wait a full three beats. ''Probably not, but we'll have to see.''

"Will you let me know how it goes? I…I won't be going around there anymore. I've decided you're right, I shouldn't be meddling in things I don't know about. But it doesn't mean I don't still care."

For the first time, a glimmer of warmth surfaced in his eyes. "I'll call you when I hear something."

"Thanks." She wanted so much to reach for him, wishing they could find comfort in each other's arms. Tod almost felt like *their* child, they both loved him so much.

"About that night we spent together…" Ben began.

A mixture of pain and joy surged through Geena at the memory, quickly squashed. "Yes?"

"It was special to me, but…"

But. "Never to be repeated," she finished for him.

"If you find yourself pregnant, be sure to tell me."

"Of course." He would do the right thing and pay maintenance; in return, she would grant him visitation rights. The scenario cut her to the quick.

"Go, or you'll miss your plane." She could feel tears welling, and she didn't want to cry, not in front of him. "Give my love and sympathy to your parents."

He descended two steps. She had a moment in which to memorize the shape of his broad shoulders and long legs before he turned and in one stride was at her side. Mutely, he put his arms around her and hugged her to him, his face in her hair. Then, before Geena knew what was happening, Ben took her mouth in a harsh, swift kiss that left her gasping.

"Ben?" She couldn't read his eyes, only sensed an anguished finality in his touch that scared her.

"I was right the first time I saw you." He stroked a tear from her cheek, and she saw that his eyes were full. "You and I are worlds apart."

"No." She cried out as he pulled away from her. "We can work things out. Ben, we just need to talk."

"Don't you get it?" he said with a low ironic laugh. "Talking only highlights our differences."

"HI, MOM. DAD." Ben fell into a three-way embrace with his parents in the airport lobby. He inhaled his mother's perfumed talc and felt like a little boy again. Until he saw the gray threading his father's dark hair and knew his parents had aged, despite how fit and tanned they looked.

"I'm so glad you could come, Ben," Elise Matthews said, getting in an extra hug. She blinked back tears and smiled at him.

"Do you need to pick up luggage from the carousel?" Tom Matthews asked, taking Ben's overnight bag from him.

Ben shook his head. The bag and Eddie's box under his arm were all he'd brought. "Let's get out of here."

They didn't talk about Eddie on their way to the house, a sprawling ranch set in the middle of a small peach orchard about twenty miles north of Austin.

"Did you get a good crop this year?" Ben asked as they drove through the orchard on the long winding driveway to the house. When his father had retired from his position as a computer engineer at IBM, he'd bought the orchard; the income supplemented his pension and provided him with a hobby.

"Too much for your mother and I to harvest," Tom told him with pride. "We had to hire pickers this year."

They didn't speak of Eddie all the way through an early dinner of barbecued chicken and salad on the back patio. Ben shed layers of clothes and soaked up the Texas sun. He wondered if other families reacted to death by ignoring it, but he knew instinctively that he and his parents needed to reestablish a strong enough connection that grief couldn't shatter them completely.

Ben talked about the snow geese, his patients, the rain and the river. He listened to gossip about his parents' neighbors, news of relatives, the price per bushel of this year's peach crop. He helped his mom clear the dishes. And all the time, Eddie's box was waiting, like an unwelcome visitor, in the foyer.

Ben was about to bring it into the living room when, out of habit, or to stave off the unpleasant task, Tom turned on the six o'clock news, as Ben knew he did every evening.

The newsreader announced a familiar name, and Ben nearly dropped the plate he was putting away.

"*Who* did he say?" Ben asked, glimpsing the Hainesville town hall decked out in flowers and banners.

"Geena Hanson, the supermodel," Tom explained. "Say, Ben, is that your Hainesville?"

"Yes." He rounded the open plan kitchen counter to stand behind the couch and watch.

"Oh, my God, there she is!" Elise left the dishwasher and joined Tom and Ben. "Do you know her, Ben?"

Ben watched Geena sway down the makeshift runway to recorded music, her smile alight, her body all long legs and fluid hips. He couldn't help but remember those same limbs wrapped around him, and his groin tightened.

"Yes," he said, entranced. "She's…she's…" A patient, a lover, a friend, a problem he couldn't solve. *She's great with kids*. In spite of her major blunder, he had to admit Tod's morale had improved out of sight since Geena had come on the scene. "She's been helping me with a patient—"

"Shh. Tell me later." Elise hushed him impatiently.

The newsreader, in mixed tones of awe and amusement, told how the news had leaked out that supermodel Geena Hanson was appearing in a charity fashion show in her tiny hometown of Hainesville and the event had been descended upon by the international media and swamped with attendees. In the images that followed, Geena lit up the camera. She was larger than life and shone with an inner fire that was more than mere beauty. Since Milan, the announcer suggested, Ms. Hanson had not only recovered, she'd gone on to greater heights.

The coverage was bound to bring modeling offers flooding in, Ben thought. If they weren't already.

When the news turned to another story, Elise sighed and nudged her son. "How come you haven't mentioned her before this? Is she dating anyone? Have you even asked her out?"

"*Mother.*" With what he hoped was an incredulous laugh, Ben averted his face from her inquisitive gaze. "She's not my type."

"What nonsense!"

They sat through the sports and the weather, still pretending this was nothing more than an impromptu weekend visit. Afterward Ben clicked the remote, and silence fell. He carried Eddie's box into the room and the smiles faded from his parents' faces. Side by side on the leather couch, Tom and Elise silently linked hands.

As Ben brought out Eddie's things, one by one, he told Tom and Elise what he could about them. His father clutched the sweatshirt, tears dripping unchecked down his jaw. "I remember him wearing this."

Elise held the clay figurine in her hands and gazed at it silently for a long time. Ben's heart squeezed tight as he watched a mother's grief for her lost son play over her face. He was surprised at what she said when she spoke at last.

"I think he's still alive." She glanced up, looking first at Tom, then at Ben.

For some strange reason, Ben thought of Geena, moving toward a light. "You mean, he's in Heaven."

"No, I simply don't believe he's dead." She dried her eyes and sat back on the couch as if making a statement: *I'm not looking through these muddy things until Eddie comes home and cleans them up.*

The image was so strong Ben almost smiled. Until he remembered that grief could unhinge the strongest mind. His mother, a retired pharmacist, had always been pragmatic; that didn't mean she couldn't break, too.

"Mom," he said gently. "Eddie's gone. It's hard to accept, but we would have heard from him by now. Every international aid organization has scoured the area."

"They haven't found his body," Elise argued.

"Elise, honey," Tom said, putting down the sweatshirt to take his wife by the other hand. "It's too late for hope. You'll only come down harder in the end."

"I don't care," she said, both obdurate and serenely confident. Scarily confident, Ben thought. "Eddie's not dead," she reiterated. "I don't know how I know, but holding that figurine I get a feeling that goes right to the bone. Eddie's coming home. Call it a mother's intuition, call me crazy if you like, but you won't get me to believe otherwise." She placed the figurine on the coffee table. "He'll be back for this."

Ben exchanged a glance with his father. "The memorial service is tomorrow, isn't it?"

Tom nodded. "It's been a long week," he said, then added with a frown at his wife, "I hope you're going to come."

"I'll come," Elise said. "Just don't expect me to cry."

She rose and hugged Ben, smiling gently at his worried expression. "I'm perfectly fine. Just tired. See you in the morning."

Tom waited until she'd left the room before leaning forward, elbows on his knees. "Your mother's been under a lot of strain. Seeing Eddie's things must have triggered something."

Ben nodded, searching for something comforting to say. "Maybe the memorial service will make his death real to her. It *is* hard, not having a...body. Maybe we're jumping the gun. It seems so soon, somehow, for a memorial service."

"Are you saying you think your mother's right?" Tom asked, looking hopeful.

Reluctantly, Ben shook his head. "If International Médicos has given up, it's highly unlikely Eddie's alive. You saw the news footage on TV. Tons of mud have buried whole villages, and buildings that missed the flooding were turned into piles of rubble by the earthquake. Thousands of bodies have yet to be identified. Many may never be. Besides, there's his backpack." Ben fingered the tattered piece of reinforced nylon. "He never went anywhere without this backpack."

Tom sighed heavily. "I guess you're right."

The memorial service was well attended; Eddie had gone to the local high school and was remem-

bered not only for his prowess on the track field but
for his debating skills and sense of humor. Hearing
his brother's achievements lauded by friend after
friend was painful for Ben. All that youthful potential, cut off by an act of God.

He shut his eyes and sank into his thoughts. Images of his brother at various stages of his life moved
through Ben's mind. Water pistols at ten paces, floating down the Colorado River on an inner tube, cheer-
ing as Eddie broke the tape at the hundred-yard dash.
Ben choked with pride as Eddie walked across the
university stage to receive his diploma from medical
school.

Other images surfaced, too. Fending off bullies
when Eddie's smart mouth got him in trouble, pig-
gybacking him home when he broke his ankle falling
off the skateboard ramp, taking his car keys off him
at a party because he'd drunk too much beer. Now
that Eddie was gone, part of Ben's reason for living
was gone. He was no longer needed to take care of
his little brother.

In a few minutes he would have to get up and give
the eulogy. He dreaded talking about Eddie, afraid
of the emotion he would go through. Afraid that acknowledging Eddie's death in words made it more
real.

Moisture seeped from beneath Ben's closed eyes,

and he squeezed them shut to keep the tears at bay. Unexpectedly, another image came into his mind. Eddie, as he'd never seen him in life, hovering high above a mountain village, his blond hair lit by a brilliant white light. Eddie's smile widened, his face suffused with joy. In a blinding flash, Eddie was made one with the light. So powerful was the image that a burst of laughter erupted from Ben's throat and tears of exultation spilled down his cheeks.

With a jolt, he came to the present. His eyes flew open, and he turned the laugh into a cough. People were looking at him. He shut his eyes again, but the vision was gone. Had it been real or just wishful thinking? Had he accepted Geena's beliefs or merely tried to comfort himself?

Brief as it was, the vision had a potent aftereffect, like a vivid dream that leaves the dreamer in the grip of strong emotions upon waking. When he stood in front of the congregation to speak of Eddie, he found his heart had lightened; he could even smile. He didn't understand it, but grief had fled. When he spoke of his brother, it was in the present tense, as if somewhere, somehow, Eddie *was* still alive.

''MERRI, COME ON, girl. Let's go for a walk.'' Geena took the lead off the hook by the back door, and the puppy scampered across the kitchen floor, her nails slipping on the linoleum in her hurry to go out. "See you in a little while, Gran."

Ruth, stirring soup at the stove, glanced out the window and shivered. Precipitation was falling; although it wasn't exactly rain, neither was it snow— it was just plain cold and wet. "Are you all packed? You have to leave for the airport in an hour, and the roads might be icy."

"I won't be long. I just want to say goodbye to someone."

"I heard Ben got back last night."

Geena turned to open the door. "I already said goodbye to him."

She put on a warm hat and buttoned her long winter coat. Treading carefully, she maneuvered down the slippery back steps, keeping a tight leash on the black bundle of canine energy dragging her downward. In her pocket was the unopened envelope containing her GED scores.

Before she rounded the house, she peeked around the corner. No reporters, thank God. In the days following the fashion show she'd received a lot of media attention. The news clips had been picked up nationwide, and Geena's agent was on the phone every day, begging her to come back to work. The agency wanted her, even though she'd gained twenty pounds since August, and there was speculation in the press

that her new look might spark a return to more vo-
luptuous models.

Kelly and Erin had laughed at that; she was still
thinner than the average American woman. Thank
God for her sisters; they kept her down to earth.
Sadly, her weight gain hadn't accomplished the one
thing she longed for. Except for some spotting a
month ago, she still hadn't had a period. She was
beginning to think she'd dreamed the whole encounter with her mother.

She walked past Tod's house and paused, looking
in at the light burning in his room. Not seeing him
was going to break her heart, but he would survive
without her. With a sigh, she hunched into her coat
and carried on through the chilly afternoon. As she
passed the high school she halted for a few moments
to watch the football team train in mud-streaked uni-
forms, their breath puffing in the cold air. She felt
her pocket and heard the stiff crinkle of the envelope.

If she had failed, she had an easy option: she could
go back to modeling as a career. If she passed, she
suddenly had choices, and life became difficult. A
tiny part of her almost hoped she had failed. Regard-
less, she would do the Dior retrospective in Paris,
then…then she'd see. *Ben.* Would it matter to him
where she was a month from now? A year?

At Greta's house, she opened the creaky gate and

walked carefully up the slippery walk. A curtain twitched in the living room. A second later, the front door opened, and a figure appeared in the porch light. "Geena. Is that you?"

"I love your outfit," Geena said, admiring the stylish cashmere pullover and matching wool pants Greta had bought by herself. The fashion show had been a real turning point for the older woman.

Greta self-consciously smoothed the pleated pants. "Come in, child. Sleet is getting inside."

Geena wiped her boots on the mat and picked Merri up so the dog wouldn't get Greta's floor dirty.

"You spoil that dog," Greta said, leading the way into the living room.

"Kelly's daughter Robyn is going to take her to obedience training next week with their puppy."

Greta's sharp eyes regarded her. "And where are you going to be?"

"I'm flying to Paris tonight for a modeling job."

"So. You're leaving us. You're leaving Ben and Tod and all those old folks who look forward to your visits so much." Greta made a tsking sound and shook her head. "Never mind. You do what you have to do. Now, how about those GED results?"

Geena handed her the envelope. "How did you know I had them?"

"I have another student who received his yesterday.'' She tore open the envelope with more tut-tutting. ''You haven't even checked your score. What's wrong with you, girl?''

She lifted her reading glasses from the chain around her neck and placed them on the end of her nose. Probably only ten seconds elapsed while she scanned the page, but to Geena it seemed an eternity. Merri licked her all over her chin, and she chipped the polish off half of her thumbnail before Greta finally glanced up.

The older woman smiled and took off her glasses. ''Congratulations. You aced it—ninety-three percent.''

Geena's jaw dropped. ''Wow. That's amazing. Let me see.'' She reached for the paper. It was true. She'd passed with flying colors. Maybe she wasn't a total moron, after all.

''So what are you going to do now?''

''I told you—I'm going to Paris.''

''I mean afterward. You can go to college, study anything you like. You work well with people. You could do social work, counseling, whatever.''

''I don't know.'' She lifted uncertain eyes to Greta. ''Lately I feel like I'm back in limbo. I don't know where I'm going.''

''It's Ben, isn't it, child?''

She nodded miserably. "It's over between us. We're too different."

Greta snorted angrily. "Who told you that?"

"He did. He thinks I'm too frivolous."

"And you believe him? If he stopped to reflect for more than a moment he'd realize how wrong he is."

Geena shook her head. "It's no use."

Greta took her hand, surprising Geena with the forcefulness of her grip. "A long time ago, I let my parents convince me the young man I loved was no good for me. I let him go, and since then I've regretted it every day of my life."

"You let him go? But I thought—"

"You probably heard the rumors that have gone around this town for decades that he jilted me." Greta sighed. "It might have been easier for me to forget if it happened that way."

"What did happen?"

Greta's mouth trembled. "I was pregnant. He wanted to marry me, but my father convinced me that would be a disaster. I told him goodbye and...and I had an abortion."

"Oh, Greta."

"That wasn't the worst of it. As a result of that botched abortion, I contracted an infection and had to have a hysterectomy. At the age of twenty-five I was faced with the prospect of never having children of my own.''

"Oh, Greta. So that's why you never married.''

Greta nodded and fell silent. "I have another confession to make,'' she said at last. "The dog that jumped out in front of your parents' car the night they went off the road was *my* dog.''

Geena would have thought nothing more that was astonishing could be revealed. "But...that was at one a.m.''

"That was the night I told my lover I'd aborted his baby. It was the night he left Hainesville and never came back. I took the dog for a walk because I couldn't sleep.'' Tears appeared in Greta's eyes. "I felt so guilty and bitter and—and *jealous* of your mother, with her three beautiful little girls, I made everyone think your father was drunk. Oh, Geena, how can you ever forgive me?''

In that instant, the kernel of resentment lodged in Geena's heart dissolved. She moved to the couch and put her arms around Greta. "Of course I forgive you. I'm so sorry for all you went through. All these years you've lived with this and no one knew.''

"Don't tell anyone,'' Greta said, dabbing at her eyes with a tissue pulled out of her sleeve. "I never meant to tell you, but you were so nice to me even when I was nasty.'' She blinked and regarded Geena curiously. ''Why were you, anyway?''

''My mom would have wanted me to be.''

''Your mother was a lovely person.'' Greta smiled through her tears. ''You remind me of her.''

Geena smiled, even though tears spilled down her cheeks. ''That's the nicest thing anyone's ever said to me.''

''Don't tell anyone what I've told you,'' Greta repeated sharply. ''I couldn't bear pity after all these years.''

''Not even my sisters?''

''I guess they deserve the truth...but you've got to swear them to secrecy.'' Greta drew in a deep breath and released it. ''And now, I hope what I've said has convinced you to give Ben another chance.''

Geena's smile faded. ''Ben needs to give *me* a chance.''

''At least talk to him,'' Greta urged. ''Try to work it out. Forget about Paris. Your whole life is at stake.''

''I can't forget Paris. I'm packed to go, my ticket is booked, people are expecting me—'' She broke off to glance at her watch. ''Oh, my God, I've got to run or I'll miss my plane.'' She hugged Greta again and kissed her on the cheek. ''Take care. Thank you for everything.''

''Thank *you*, my dear.''

CHAPTER FIFTEEN

"I'M SORRY, Ben, she's gone." Ruth Hanson gazed apologetically at him through her oversize glasses.

"Gone," he repeated, unable to comprehend. "Simcoe? Seattle?"

"Paris. She took a modeling job."

Desolation hit him hard between the ribs. He'd counted on seeing her, had rushed straight from the airport to her house before he'd gone home. "Did she leave any message for me?"

"I'm sorry," Ruth said again, looking distressed. "I can give you her cell phone number. She's hard to get hold of, though, what with the time difference and the fact that she sleeps till noon and is awake half the night."

Ben copied the number on a scrap of paper and tucked it in his wallet. "When is she coming back?"

"She wasn't sure. She said she might go to London next."

A wriggling bundle of black fur shot between Ruth's track-suited legs and launched itself at Ben.

"Good girl, Merri," he said, absently scratching behind the dog's ears.

"I hope she won't go back to her old ways," Ruth fretted. "Not eating, taking pills…"

Ben shook his head. "I'm sure she won't. She's got her head screwed on right." And for how long had he been so sure she didn't? "Thanks, Ruth. I'll call her."

"Good luck, son. She needs to feel wanted for herself."

He winced. "I know."

GEENA SAT in a bistro on the Champs-Elysée with a glass of Ricard and water and opened the envelope her agent had forwarded to her. It was a card from Tod, which he'd made himself. On the front he'd drawn fighter planes raining fiery missiles onto an armored tank. A huge explosion colored in with red and orange fire presumably depicted another tank that had been blown up. Typical nine-year-old boy. But if the outside made her smile, the inside brought her tears. He'd drawn a picture of her, a stilt-legged creature with a neck a giraffe would be proud of, holding hands with a bald-headed boy sprouting a few strands of hair. A red love heart beat in the boy's T-shirt, roughly in the vicinity of the stomach.

Printed below in pencil, the caption read, "What's a wok?"

She smiled. *I give up, Tod.*

Following the arrow she turned the page, and there was the answer. "A thing you thwow at wabbits."

Geena laughed until she cried. And then she couldn't stop crying. She missed Tod so much. She wouldn't have left him if Ben hadn't told her to. But she'd learned something about forgiveness from Greta, and if she could forgive a former enemy, she could surely forgive the man she loved.

AT FIVE MINUTES to six that Friday, as Ben was about to leave his house for the Burger Shack, his phone rang. He stared at it, goose bumps rising on his neck and arms. Eddie?

Finally he realized it had rung seven or eight times and lunged at it, knocking it almost off the desk in his hurry. "Hello?"

"Ben?"

"*Geena.*" Joy swiftly replaced disappointment, to be followed instantly by grievance. "I've been trying to get hold of you all week. Why haven't you returned my calls?"

"Because you're not awake when I am. If you're going to accost me, I'll hang up."

Whoa, she was in a feisty mood. "Okay…"

"I've been doing a lot of thinking and I've got a thing or two to tell you."

He had an idea what she was going to say, but maybe he needed to hear it. She certainly deserved to say it. "Shoot."

"I will, but first, how is Tod?"

"He went in yesterday for another round of chemo. He's feeling pretty sick, but he's stoic. I promised him a trip to the Burger Shack when he's up to it. Oh, and he loved the joke book and other presents you had delivered to him."

She let out a deep sigh. "Good. Now, Ben…"

Here it comes. He leaned back in the beanbag and tucked his toes under Ursula's warm belly.

"All I ever did was offer Tod and his mother my friendship, sympathy and whatever practical assistance I could render. I didn't tell Carrie to stop treatment. I wasn't responsible for her interpretation of my innocent wish that Tod would become well again. I might not be qualified to counsel cancer patients, but I love that boy. Surely that means something."

"Yes—"

"You told me to stay away, but I don't have to obey you like you're some kind of god. Self-confidence is something I have to work on but when it comes to Tod, I *know* I have something to offer. Doctors can pump him full of all the medicines in the world, but they can't duplicate the healing power of a loving heart.''

''I know that now,'' he agreed quietly.

''And another thing— What did you say?''

Lord, he wished she wasn't thousands of miles away speaking from the other end of a telephone line. If he could take her in his arms maybe everything would be okay.

He drew a deep breath and let it out. ''I'm a doctor. My whole purpose in life is to heal. I love Tod, too, and that makes it all the more important to me that he be cured. The fact is, I was afraid of what I didn't understand, afraid that the best efforts of medicine might not be able to cure Tod.'' He halted. ''I was jealous of you, of your serenity in the face of death, jealous of the possibility you might have a bigger role in Tod's recovery than science. If I as a doctor can't cure disease, I've lost a big part of my reason for being. I know all this is somewhat irrational. My thoughts are unworthy of a doctor—or of a human being, for that matter.''

''Ben—''

''Finally—and this is the crux of the matter and unbelievably hard to admit—you forced me to confront myself, to realize that maybe I'm not as enlightened and open-minded as I thought.''

There was such a long pause he wondered if they'd lost the connection. "Geena?"

"I think you are, after all," she said. "Accepting something that challenges your belief system isn't easy. If I hadn't experienced near death I would have found the phenomenon hard to believe, too. The books I've read on the subject say that marriages and family relationships often break down after one person has a near-death experience because his or her life and worldview changes so dramatically."

He sighed heavily. "Science doesn't explain everything in life, nor should we expect it to."

"So I'm right and you're wrong? Can I get that in writing?"

He heard the teasing note and breathed a sigh of relief. She was going to let him off easy. "In blood, if necessary. While I'm on the floor groveling, I should tell you that your account of your near-death experience helped me deal with grief over Eddie. The weird thing is, as soon as I accepted his death, I immediately started to believe he was alive. I'm not sure if I believe it metaphorically or literally, but on some level I know you're right."

Her voice softened. "Thank you for understanding and accepting...and for saying so. It means the world to me."

"*You* mean the world to me, Geena. When will you be home?"

"I...I don't know. I'm going to New York after the show finishes. I have to see someone, do some things."

"I see." But he didn't see at all. Was she ever coming back? They'd covered so much sensitive ground that at the moment he lacked the courage to ask. "Say, did you ever get your GED results?"

"Yes. I got ninety-three percent."

"I always knew you'd do well."

"But Ben? I've decided...I'm not going to college."

He was stunned into silence. In the back of his mind he'd been counting on her taking up a new career, perhaps in some field of social work. At any rate, a career that would fit into his life. He'd always assumed he'd marry someone like Penny, the British nurse he'd known in Guatemala, earnest, dedicated and caring. Not anymore.

Geena was dedicated and caring, plus she had an extra layer to her that was the icing on the cake. What he'd once called frivolity he recognized as irrepressible zest for life. But what he hadn't expected, and hated the thought of, was that Geena might return to flitting around the world. If that made him a selfish jerk, then she'd caused him to learn something else about himself.

"Why not?" he said at last.

"It's not me. I know you're disappointed."

"I have no right to be disappointed." He needed to prove himself worthy of *her*. "It's what you want that counts. Above all things, even my own selfish desires, I want you to be happy."

"Thank you."

"So...I guess I'll see you when I see you." There was another pause. Ben added, "You know how you didn't want me to say it until I was ready? I'm ready now. I love you, Geena." There was no response. "Am I too late with this?"

She hadn't answered because she was crying. "It's never too late to tell someone you love her, Ben."

Which was true, but it didn't answer his question.

GEENA BOARDED the flight from New York to Seattle with some trepidation. If, after all she and Ben had been through, she'd misinterpreted his remarks or miscalculated by not telling him her news on the phone, she would never forgive herself. But as the plane lifted off and she got that lighter-than-air rush in her stomach, she let excitement overtake concern. Tonight she would see him. She'd missed Ben so much, and they had so much to say to each other. She hoped he would be as happy as she was.

It was Friday, and by the time she drove into Hainesville, darkness had fallen over the town. Ben would soon be finished work, if he wasn't already. She thought about casually meeting him at the Burger Shack but decided she couldn't wait and went straight to the clinic.

The waiting room was empty, and Barbara, the receptionist, was putting on her coat. "Geena!" she exclaimed. "When did you get back?"

"Just now." She glanced toward the examining room. "Is Ben still here?"

"He's finishing up some paperwork." Barbara bustled across the room and knocked on Ben's door with a conspiratorial grin at Geena. "Someone to see you, Dr. Matthews."

"Send him in," came his abstracted reply.

That was Ben; he would never turn anyone away, no matter how late, no matter how tired he was.

Barbara left the door ajar and nodded at Geena. "Go on. I'm off home."

Geena stood a moment in the doorway looking at him. Head bent, hair tousled from running his fingers through it, his fountain pen moving across the paper with a faint scratching sound. Slowly she crossed the room, avoiding a stack of cardboard cartons.

"Be with you in a moment," he murmured, still not looking up. Then he paused, breathed in, and she knew he'd caught the scent of her perfume. His head came up. "Geena!"

"Hello, Ben." Heart tripping, she forced herself not to fling herself straight into his arms and instead dropped casually into a chair and crossed one leg over the other. They'd come full circle, back to where they'd begun.

His gaze slid down her leg where it emerged, slender and pale, from the gap in her long winter coat and come to rest on the high-heeled shoe dangling from her toes. Capping his pen, he leaned back in his chair. "I didn't know you were back."

All the way across the Atlantic Ocean, all the way across the country, Geena had comforted, amused and tortured herself recalling the exact color of his eyes, the cleft in his chin, the breadth of his shoulders and springiness of his hair. The feel of his hands on her skin.

She tipped her head to one side and inspected her nails. "I have an appointment. You insisted two months ago on a follow-up examination."

"Right." He glanced over his desk. "Your file doesn't seem to be here. Hang on. I'll go get it."

Dear Ben.

He was back in seconds, dropping the open file on

his desk, slinging his stethoscope around his neck, reaching for the blood pressure cuff.

Geena rose, shrugging out of her fur-trimmed coat, letting it slide to the chair beneath her. Ben swallowed visibly. She'd given a lot of thought to what she would wear for their reunion. The dress was from the fall collection she'd modeled, a silky, slinky knit that draped the softened angles of her new curvaceous figure. Her breasts were fuller, too; would he notice?

She slid the sleeve above her elbow, exposing her bare skin. He looked as though he wanted to start at the inside wrist and kiss his way up her tender inner arm. Her body warmed and melted at the thought.

"Well?" She moved closer, thrusting her arm under his nose. "Aren't you going to take my blood pressure?"

With unsteady hands, Ben strapped the cuff around her upper arm and pumped it up. "How's Ruth?"

"I haven't been home yet."

His gaze shot up. She smiled, acknowledging the significance of coming first to him.

"You're looking well," he said.

She arched a brow. "Is that your professional opinion?"

He grinned wryly. "At the moment I'm having trouble remembering if I'm a man or a doctor."

"They're not mutually exclusive," she murmured, but wasn't sure he heard, because he'd tucked the ends of the stethoscope in his ears and was concentrating on listening to her heart pumping blood.

"Blood pressure's fine." He lifted his fingers to her neck and, with gentle pressure, felt the glands beneath her jaw.

She caught his gaze. Heat surged between them, and she parted her lips, willing him to kiss her. Flustered, he dropped his hands and reached again for his stethoscope. She leaned forward slightly so he could slip it beneath the top of her dress. His breath fanned over her. The stethoscope was cold, his fingers warm.

"Your heart rate's a little high." His mouth curved. "White coat syndrome?"

"Ben Matthews syndrome."

His smile widened. "Step on the scales, please."

She slipped off her shoes and climbed onto the scales, giving him a flirtatious glance over her shoulder. "I wouldn't do this for any man but you."

"You've gained—" he leaned back to consult her medical records "—twenty-three pounds." His eyebrows rose. "Have your periods returned?"

"No."

He frowned. "I don't know why not. Maybe your body fat index isn't high enough yet."

She had to bite her inner cheek to stop herself from smiling with smug satisfaction. "Maybe."

"When did you last have a complete gynecological examination?"

"Last week in New York."

"Did the doctor have any ideas about why you're still experiencing amenorrhea?"

"She had a theory. How's Ursula?"

He blinked at the sudden change of topic. "Fine. I don't know how she's going to adapt when I move to Austin, but..."

Geena's bubbling spirits lost their fizz. "Austin? I thought you were going to ask Dr. Cameron if he wanted a partner."

His gaze had an intensity that made her unable to look away. "With Eddie gone, my parents are feeling lost. I'd like to spend some time with them."

Somberly, she nodded. "I understand. After Milan, all I wanted to do was go home to my family who loved me. What about Tod?"

"I'll keep in close touch." He paused. "What are your plans?"

She shrugged. She was biting her lip to keep from crying. He'd said he loved her; why was this happening? "Nothing firm yet. I just want to be around people who need my help. I'm lucky enough to have money. I don't require a paying job."

She stared at him, waiting for him to speak. Hadn't she given him enough clues? They seemed to exist in suspended animation, emotion shimmering in the air around them, unable to burst into life.

In nightmarish slow motion, she reached for her coat. He helped her on with it. With a sigh, she started to walk away.

Behind her, he cleared his throat. "Geena?"

She paused, and he closed the distance between them. When he put his hands on her shoulders, hope sprang to her heart. "Yes, Ben?"

He turned her to face him, and the love in his eyes convinced her that all was not lost. That, in fact, everything that mattered had been found.

"Will you marry me?"

"I thought you'd never ask." She melted into his arms, letting out a sigh of heartfelt relief when his arms closed around her. Finally, they were together, and this time nothing would part them.

"Ben?" she murmured, pulling away after a moment. "There's something I have to tell you."

"Hmm." His mouth captured hers, distracting her. Sometime later, she tried again.

"Remember I said the gynecologist had a theory?"

"Huh? Oh." His voice lost its fuzziness as he became alert to a possible medical condition. "What was it?"

"What's the most common reason for a woman to stop having periods?"

He shook his head, shrugged. "Pregnancy, but—"

She grinned.

Understanding dawned. "Are you— You mean, you're pregnant?" he spluttered.

She pressed a finger against his chest. "*We* are pregnant." She contemplated his stunned expression. "Are you okay with that?"

With a whoop, he gathered her into his arms and spun her around. "I'm more than okay—I'm ecstatic. Oh, man, this is so great." He set her on her feet and grinned at her. "You're sure?"

With an answering smile, she nodded. "In Paris, I had a feeling something was different about my body. So I got a pregnancy testing kit, and sure enough the stick turned blue. My gynecologist in New York confirmed it." She paused, slanting up a sly glance. "Can I say it?"

"Okay, okay." With a teasing smile, he rolled his eyes. "Your mom was right. Sheesh." He kissed her again, long enough to melt her bones. Then drew away to give her a hard stare. "But let's get one thing straight—this is not some sort of immaculate conception. *I* was there."

She laughed. "Did you think I would forget? Come on, I want to go tell Gran."

"Okay, I guess I'm done here. It's past six o'clock." His gaze dropped, the light of happiness briefly dimmed.

Friday night. He was thinking of Eddie. Geena quickly kissed him again. "Later, we can go to the Burger Shack and you won't even have to prod me to eat. I'm starving."

He put on his coat and linked her arm through his, whispering all the things he wanted to do with her as soon as they were alone.

The phone rang.

He glanced at it, hope springing to his face only to be quickly suppressed. "Leave it to the answering machine. I'm too happy tonight to set myself up for disappointment."

"Okay," she said reluctantly. Ordinarily she had no problem not answering phones, but something about that ring called her insistently. Eight rings, nine…

At the door, Geena broke away and ran to pick up the phone. "Hello?" She paused to listen. "Oh, my God!"

Ben, frozen to the spot at the door, stared at her. His voice strangely tight, he said, "Who is it? Is it Tod?"

She waved him over, kicked out a chair and, holding her hand over the receiver, ordered, "Sit."

"Who is it?"

"Sit down."

His eyes gripped hers as he lowered himself into the chair. She handed him the phone, her voice on the threshold between tears and laughter.

"It's Eddie. He says reports of his death have been greatly exaggerated."

EPILOGUE

MERRI, ecstatic at being let off the leash, dashed up and down the riverbank, plowing through layers of dead leaves beneath trees sprouting summer greenery. The year-old puppy stopped abruptly, sides heaving, waiting for Ursula to catch up before dashing off again.

Tod ran after the dogs, flinging sticks with abandon, his blond hair waving in the summer breeze. He'd been in remission for two months, and his doctors were optimistic about his prognosis.

Geena adjusted the weight of her burden and turned to check that Ben and his brother were still coming. Eddie was here on a week's leave before going back to Guatemala. He and Ben hadn't stopped talking since Eddie's arrival yesterday, going over the disaster in Guatemala and the details of Eddie's disappearance in the mountains.

"Why didn't you get word to someone you were still alive?" Ben said. "We were all worried sick."

Eddie frowned. "Remember that pregnant girl I'd

gone to check on? We'd left her village and were coming down the mountain when the earthquake hit. We had to leave the trail because of the mud slides and ended up going miles around the far side of the mountain. We found shelter in a hut, but we were stranded, cut off by landslides. I lost my backpack crossing the flooding river.''

Ben shook his head. ''When I saw that backpack I thought you must be dead, because I knew you would never leave it.''

''Hey, it snagged on a submerged tree branch and threatened to pull me under. I let it go without a second's hesitation.''

''When the flooding receded, why didn't you come back?''

''By then there was no way the girl could undertake the journey. I couldn't abandon her while she needed medical attention. But I'll tell you, delivering that baby safely in the midst of death and destruction was a high I'll never forget.''

Ben clapped his brother on the back. ''Life goes on, one way or another. We have to celebrate it every day.''

''Amen to that. You've got good cause for celebration.''

Geena, listening, suspected Eddie was referring to her and the baby, and Ben confirmed it. ''Wait till the woman you love gives birth to your child, little bro. There's nothing like it in the world.''

Geena gazed at the peaceful face of her sleeping daughter, snug in the baby carrier. ''We're so lucky, you and I, Sonja,'' she whispered. ''You've got the best daddy in the world, and I've got a man I will love forever.'' She lifted her gaze to the blue heights of the summer sky. ''Love you, Mom. And Dad.'' And Gramps. And Gran, Erin, Kelly and all the nieces and husbands and all her friends, young and old. She had so much in life to be thankful for.

Behind her, she heard Ben carry on in a more teasing vein to Eddie. ''You missed a hell of a fine memorial service. I don't know if I'll ever be as eloquent on the subject of your demise again.''

Eddie punched him in the arm. ''Put your speeches away, buddy. I'm not planning on checking out any time soon.''

They started wrestling like two kids, then Eddie ran ahead, tagging Tod on the shoulder, before chasing the dogs.

Ben caught up to Geena and put his arm around her. ''How're my girls?''

''We're just fine. It's great to meet Eddie. He's exactly how I imagined. When are your parents coming up? We haven't seen them since the wedding.''

"They'll be here on Friday, in time for the christening."

"Are you sorry we didn't go to live in Austin after all?"

"It's okay. Once we knew Eddie was safe there wasn't the same impetus to move—although I'm never going to let more than a few months go between visits. Luckily Brent Cameron agreed that the practice needed another doctor."

"Well, *I'm* glad we stayed. We got to see Tod get well."

"And thanks to you and Greta, the ladies' auxiliary raised enough money with the spring fashion show to make a start on the maternity wing."

"I was hoping it would be built in time for Sonja, but I expect there will be more babies."

"Damn right there will be." Ben stopped and lifted her chin to kiss her lightly on the lips. "Carrie *still* thinks you're an angel."

"What do *you* think?" she teased. "Or shouldn't I ask?"

"You're much too human to be an angel." He slanted his mouth across hers and deepened the kiss, until heat rushed through her and her heart was slamming against her ribs. With a twinkle in his eye for their bedroom hijinks, he murmured, "Thank God for that."

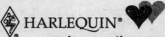

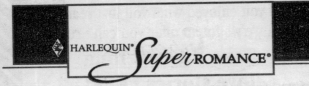